Firel

Also available by K.M. Peyton
in Scholastic Press:

Unquiet Spirits

Firehead

K.M. Peyton

SCHOLASTIC
PRESS

Scholastic Children's Books,
Commonwealth House, 1–19 New Oxford Street,
London WC1A 1NU, UK
a division of Scholastic Ltd
London ~ New York ~ Toronto ~ Sydney ~ Auckland

First published in the UK by Scholastic Ltd, 1998

Copyright © K.M. Peyton, 1998

ISBN 0 590 19389 9

Typeset by DP Photosetting, Aylesbury, Bucks.
Printed by Cox and Wyman Ltd, Reading, Berks.

10 9 8 7 6 5 4 3 2 1

The right of K.M. Peyton to be identified as the author of this work has
been asserted by her in accordance with the Copyright, Designs and
Patents Act, 1988.

Chapter 1

Fate did not smile kindly on Edmund Fire-head. An impetuous boy, as his name implied, by running too fast in his excitement he failed to see an old ox-yoke that was lying on the path into the settlement, tripped over and crashed awkwardly to the ground. A fearsome pain shot up his leg into his very guts and took his breath away. He screamed out in agony.

"That's your bone broken," his brother said, hearing the disturbance.

A gaggle of women crowded round and the old granny who knew about these things was pushed forward.

"Carry him indoors," she said to his brother.

"I saw – I saw – " gasped Ed.

But as his brother picked him up he screamed and fainted.

When he came to, he was aware only of the

pain. He was on his own straw pallet on the earth floor of their hut. The granny had tied his whole leg up to an axe haft with tight bindings, and thrown a couple of sheepskins over him. He could not move. His mother looked down at him bitterly, biting her lip. She would have to do his work, and there was a new baby at her breast.

He tried to remember, moaning.

"I saw – " The words faded. It had been a dream, with the pain, of a ship with a dragon's head sliding through the fog. But the sound of the oars had not been a dream. So even, so quiet, so evil.

"I saw a ship – "

"Be quiet. You must rest and keep still," said his mother.

The old granny came and made him drink some foul brew which sent him to sleep. When he awoke the sun was shining strongly into the hut through the opening and he could see that – now – it was spring. He could smell it. The hut was built in a pit of earth, extended above with stakes and woven wattles filled with clay. The roof over his head, made of boughs and leaves and straw and skins and anything his brother thought might keep out some of the rain, let through chinks of bright sunlight. But there had been fog...

"I saw a ship."

"Oh, stop blathering," said his brother. "You've got a fever. You must lie quiet."

Edmund lay quiet. He was frightened of his brother. His father had got hit with an axe when serving under King Aethelred and his two eldest brothers had gone to fight the Norsemen in York and never returned. Since then the sixteen-year-old Oswy had been more or less the head of the family. The heart had gone out of their father, with his wound and his age, and Oswy now made the decisions. Such as they were.

"Feed the pig."

"Set the bird trap."

"Mend the fence."

"Fetch a sack of flour from Sigewulf."

"Make a new haft for the shovel."

"Get some more reeds for the roof."

"Go and get some driftwood for the fire."

He had been getting driftwood ... on the shore. A thick fog had been lying over the sea. Ed drifted in his fever, remembering the distant sound beyond the fog, a faint splash, pause, splash – almost a whisper. A voice. A *voice*? He had crouched back in the reeds, waiting, still as a heron, hardly breathing.

"I heard – I heard oars –"

"Oh, do shut up."

His sisters had been sent for the driftwood instead and had seen nothing, save the fog which still lay over the water. There was often fog in the spring. When it was clear you could see the far side of the river mouth two miles away, and the open water that was called the German ocean. The invaders came from across the German ocean. But Ed had never seen any yet. Only heard the tales. They came from rocky, snowbound shores more than a hundred miles away in ships rowed by forty men. Open ships with prows that reared high in a great carved dragon's head to look where it was going. And at the stern a man stood on a platform holding the handle of a steering-board that trailed behind, making a spume on the water which came floating into the shore at the ship's passing. And the man had only been a boy, not much older than himself (eleven), in a blue tunic, with long yellow hair and a gold torque round his neck, and eyes as blue as the sky.

Ed drifted in his delirium, the memory losing itself in the mist that blotted out his brain as well as the German ocean.

He was unconscious when the messenger came to the settlement, agape with his tale of death and disaster. He had run five miles and had blood on his clothes and terror in his eyes.

4

"Fifty men, with swords and axes – they killed the elders and the children and took the men and women captive. They want the settlement. They have set up camp and will defend it, and then go inland to find horses and cattle. They will come here – soon. Very soon. When they have slept and eaten."

Fifty men! There were no more than fifteen or twenty in the settlement five miles away, and half those women and children.

Oswy told his father they must go.

"I don't want to be a slave, nor the girls either!"

"How can we go with Edmund unconscious?" said his mother.

"Do you want your baby killed, and the girls taken by the Norsemen? Of course we must go," Oswy shouted at her. "Ed can be left where he is. Asser will stay and look after him."

Asser was so old that death would do him a good turn.

His mother looked down at the limp form of her youngest son on his straw bed and cried because she knew that Oswy was right. She had three little girls younger than Edmund and a husband who needed shielding. If they all went with Oswy they stood a chance. Oswy was forceful and strong and knew the way to safety. They had an old uncle who lived behind the defences of Lundenburg fifty miles away. Oswy had been there as a child with his father, and swore he could lead them back there.

"It's the only chance, mother! You heard what's happened! They will be here by the next daylight. You cannot risk us all for the sake of crazy Ed!"

No, but Edmund was her darling, her Firehead with his burning orange curls and his quickfire nature. None of her other children had his orange hair and nor did her husband. Only his mother knew where the remarkable colour came from. Her husband had been away from home for four years, loyal to their useless king until the axe blow felled him. She in her loneliness had fallen under the spell of a travelling Celtic minstrel. He had sung with the voice of a sea-god and plucked such tunes from his funny little Roman lyre that she had fallen in love with him. Him or his music, she never knew. She had never heard music before or since, and dreamed of it sometimes when she lay on her pallet and watched the stars through the chinks in the reeds. (Oh, how their roof leaked!) Her husband, so pleased to be home, never remarked on the fact that she had a year-old child when he had been away four times the child's age. The axe blow had addled him. And the child enchanted him, so funny and quick and golden, unlike the older boys with their dark brows and aggressive characters. Edmund Firehead he was called, as leaping and quick as his name.

But now he was to be left to the invaders.

She leaned over him and wept, the hot tears falling on his stony face and closed eyelids. The broken bone had set up a blood poisoning and the granny doctor said he would die.

"Leave him! Hurry away and save your other children. Oswy is right. This boy is as good as dead, invaders or no invaders."

A fractured bone often meant death or, if not, disablement. Only one better than having one's hands cut off by the Norsemen.

Oswy set his mother to packing her few belongings and piling them on the ox. He hoped the pig might come with them – the girls could drive it with sticks. Nobody had a horse out where they lived on the marshes. There were no rich settlements nearer than Maldon twelve miles away and, even there, only the rich thanes owned horses. Oswy looked down on Edmund's still form when he was ready to leave and was moved by a pang of pity – the little devil, to be so unlucky! Fit, he would have been a valuable companion, so full of energy and invention. Oswy, not quite sure which god he answered to – Christian, pagan or even Norse – commended his brother to them all to be on the safe side, and made the sign of the cross over him. His mother had taught him that. He had no idea what it meant. But the gods decided everything and one had to keep in favour.

Then his mother came, crying her eyes out, and he had to harden himself to chivvy her out, and turn his back on Edmund.

The old man Asser stood in the doorway wringing his hands.

"See to him, Asser. If he gets better bring him to my uncle's house in Lundenburg. It lies on the Walbrook stream, by the new church. If we go elsewhere, we'll leave word there."

But he knew Edmund wouldn't get better. And he didn't care what happened to Asser. Asser was reputed to be a hundred years old but everyone knew that wasn't possible. His father, he said, had seen King Alfred. If the story was true, then indeed he was old. But Oswy couldn't count, save by his fingers, for the sheep.

They left before dusk, to travel by night. Everybody in the village left, save Asser and Edmund Firehead.

*

The sea-fog lifted and the spring tide lapped softly on the shore. The stars came out and far away upstream the fires burned on the shore where the Norsemen had landed.

A boy with long blond hair and sky-blue eyes stood watching the sparks flying up to join the stars. He stayed apart from the drinking and the singing and the carousing. He wanted to hold on to this enormous excitement that wrapped him round, that made him tremble. To have crossed the German Ocean – at last! – to be on the land that all the tales were told of! To be where his father and his grandfather had fought, where his brothers had made home, where all the riches were for the taking! Their own king, Sven Forkbeard, had conquered nearly all this British kingdom. The weak British king was about to flee to France. And his own father Ragnar had sailed to Britain to make a home for his wife and sons when the fighting was done. And he had brought his youngest son with him because he had pleaded so hard. "You are too young to fight! Only twelve! You'll have to prove yourself."

And he had proved himself, and shown his father, and stayed on the steering-board even when the ship had taken great waves on board and tried to broach to. He had been wet through for days and his arms and back had ached as if he had been flogged. But he had never given in, or made a murmur of complaint. And now he was standing here on this beach, and the sea was gentle and the far shore lay like a dark cloak under the glitter of the spring sky. How well he knew those stars now! The stars he had seen go round from bow to stern, from horizon to horizon, all save the fixed Northern star, the one he had steered by . . . to come to England.

He stood in the dark, alone, thanking his god Thor for bringing him here safely. Whatever might happen, this was the great adventure he had longed for ever since he could remember. How it would turn out was up to greater powers than his own.

Chapter 2

When he opened his eyes, Edmund was aware of a strange silence. There was a terrible pain in the right side of his body, yet that did not worry him as much as the silence. He knew he was on his own bed in his own home, but there was no feel of home around him. Only a great emptiness. No children shouting, no sound of hens or sheep, no arguing, nothing.

He could not move. He lay trying to remember.

It came back to him slowly. The ship he had seen in the mist ... himself running, falling over the yoke ... the pain. But where had everyone gone? How long had he lain in his bed? The bed stank. He was desperately thirsty. Where was his mother? Why wasn't she there to look after him when he needed her?

His head ached, yet his brain was clear. The

ship in the mist had been no figment of his imagination. He knew that. The ship had been carrying invaders. It couldn't have gone much farther up the river without running aground, so perhaps they had come ashore and destroyed the village, and butchered his family and friends. Under the covers, they would have missed him. How long had he lain in his sleep of sickness?

There were no answers to his rambling. The sun, at least, was shining. The birds were singing and a cow lowed gently from the direction of the river. Not all life was extinct.

Then old Asser came in, and exclaimed with astonishment at seeing him alive.

"You slept the sleep of the dead! I swore to your mother that I would look over you, but they all thought you would die."

"And the Norsemen?"

"They have not come yet, but their camp is on the shore by the white shingle. I saw their fires last night. And on the wind I could hear their voices. They sang, and then they slept. They will come soon, looking for beasts and fuel. Everyone – your family – has left, making west, to save themselves."

"And me?" Abandoned by Oswy and his own mother, left to the invaders! They had swords, sharp on both sides, with hafts inlaid with silver and tips stained with blood. They killed everyone in their path, or else took them as slaves.

"I will hear them coming," Asser said. "We will lie low, under the covers. They will pass us by, do not fear."

Do not fear! Idiot man! But fear was to be overcome. His eldest brother Wistan had shown no fear when the elders of the village had accused him of stealing and made him walk over burning embers to prove his innocence. He had walked slowly, his head up, his blue eyes full of scorn for their lies. The elders had been humbled. "God has proved him innocent," they proclaimed piously. But afterwards Wistan's feet had broken into the most terrible blisters, and he had had to walk about as normal and do his work, pretending he was unharmed. Yet the pain had been terrible. Ed remembered with awe Wistan's courage. Not to limp. To stride out, smile, laugh. Ed had worshipped Wistan, the eldest. He missed him terribly. When tales of Sven Forkbeard's slaughter had filtered south, Wistan and Godric had gone to fight against him. They had never been heard of since. Godric was a stalwart boy, like Oswy. Without Wistan's flame. Wistan was sixteen when he had departed two years ago, and Godric a year younger.

So, I have lost all my family and friends and am helpless with a broken leg. Ed stared at the sky through the holes in the roof. The invaders – killers – are on their way. I cannot move. Asser says do not fear. I am worse off than a tethered pig. But I must not fear. How do you not fear? How did you stop your body quivering at the thought of the killers coming in at the door, perhaps with oil-soaked rushes flaming to torch the poor hovel. He had heard all the stories. He clenched his hands, remembered Wistan.

Asser was useless, unless he had a chance to argue with his silver tongue. But they spoke another language! Asser was a scholar of a sort. He could recite long poems, and knew about the Romans and King Alfred. But he could not read or write like the holy man at Othona. He could tell tales, but he could not write them. Nobody could. And they could only count to as many sheep as they possessed – not far. Even Wistan.

"Perhaps we can bribe them," Asser said. "Offer them what they want, to let us in peace."

"We haven't got anything." Edmund propped himself on one elbow and looked round the bare hut. Oswy had taken everything useful, and their only valuable, the ox.

14

"They accept bribery, we know that," Asser said bitterly.

"The king gives them gold to go away," Ed agreed. Everyone knew that. They went away, then next year came back for more, laughing. The country was bled dry. And still they killed and slaughtered, even as they took the money. They retreated, laughing and killing and stacking the gold in their proud ships to sail home.

"Their country is cold and full of rocks. They want to settle here. Who can blame them?" Asser said.

Ed could not picture another country. He had stood on the shore and looked and looked, and seen only the line of the sea meeting the line of the sky. He knew it was warmer in the south, and colder in the north. He knew the north and south from the sun in the day and the stars at night. That was all. He could not picture a land of rocks. There were no rocks where he lived. Just marsh and shingle and scrub and trees. Wistan and Godric had gone north. Were there rocks there, perhaps? He had no idea.

Asser brought him some water and, later, some milk. There were still a couple of old cows to be milked, and a flock of hens; they would not starve. But as the sun moved away from the holes in the roof and the golden smell of the marsh afternoon drifted into the hut, they heard voices from the direction of the river – distant at first, and then louder. The invaders had slept off their journey.

"They may come in peace, who knows?" Asser muttered.

Ed raised himself up to watch the doorway. The pain in his leg was intense. Remember Wistan. Wistan had smiled, walking slowly over the glowing firepit.

The voices drew nearer, loud and jovial, rough. Laughing. Victors.

Asser drew back into the hut, muttering. He looked to Ed suddenly very old and frail, and frightened. A young voice shouted, and then a deeper one, very abrupt, commanding. The doorway darkened. The commanding voice filled it – a man very tall, taller than Wistan, with cruel eyes the colour of stones, hay-coloured hair worn long and carelessly, a nose like a headland. In his hand he carried a sword. It gleamed gold and silver, made pretty by engraved patterns down the shaft, but with blood dripping from the tip.

Asser threw out his arms to show that he was no enemy, but the sword went between them, straight into his heart. Asser choked on his own blood, making a horrible, gargling noise, and fell in a heap like a bundle of old clothes thrown down. Ed tried to spring up, unthinking, and fell in a similar heap, his makeshift splint tipping him asprawl with a pain that put bravery out of his head. The sword gleamed by his head. He could smell the blood. Between the great bony fingers gripping the haft, small red and blue jewels peeped out as if to witness the action. The next death. He shut his eyes. It would be quick, if Asser was anything to go by. His hot, coursing bloodstream froze in that second.

But another voice cut in, lighter than the murderer's, scarcely broken. Another person, a boy, shoved the hand holding the sword unceremoniously to one side. Ed opened his eyes in time to see the imperious gesture. A boy his own age with the look of the older man, but unformed. Not a murderer yet, perhaps. A smile. Ed's heart sprang with hope.

The boy said something to the swordsman in a warm, eager voice. He pointed to Ed, put out a hand and ran it over Ed's fiery curls. He laughed. Ed gathered that his firehead was attracting attention as usual, this time perhaps to his advantage. Although he could not understand the conversation it was clear that the boy wanted Ed's life spared because the colour of his hair appealed to him. He said something to his brother – it must be his brother – that Ed was pretty sure meant he wanted him saved. The brother's sword was – although pushed aside – still raised, and the huge bony fingers tightened on the haft. If it came down from that direction, Ed reckoned his head would be sliced right off. He stiffened, willing Wistan's heart into his own. He could feel the sweat bathing his body from the pain in his leg. Then the boy spoke more sharply, bossily. Whatever he said, the sword was drawn back.

And then he said something else, which this time Ed understood. "I want him. He is mine. He will be my slave."

His brother lifted his sword again and smacked Ed's leg excruciatingly with the side of the blade. He said, "The boy is useless. What do you want with a broken body?"

The younger boy turned a fierce gaze on his brother and argued sharply. He was no tame sibling. The man shrugged and laughed, but turned away without pursuing the argument. He stepped over Asser's body lying on the floor as if it were one of the tumbled blankets. Edmund looked at the body with the blood flowing out of its mouth and nose, and resisted the terror that threatened to take hold. He was alone now, terribly. At the mercy of this youth who liked the colour of his hair. What a slender hold on life!

The boy did not follow his brother. He threw one of the sacks over Asser, hiding the body, not looking at it. Perhaps, like Edmund, he had not seen many violent deaths – yet. Then he turned his back on the body and came over to Ed. He smiled down at him. Against the light his blond hair made a halo round his head. He wore a thick-woven tunic of sea-blue wool, stained and muddied, and a heavy gold necklace such as Ed had never seen. His face was strong for a boy's, with the family's hawkish nose and the eyes as blue as his tunic, but its expression was not hostile.

He pointed to himself and said a word that sounded like "Rollo". He repeated it several times and then pointed to Ed and raised his eyebrows.

Edmund said his name, presuming that was what was wanted, and Rollo smiled and repeated it. It was a common enough name, after all. Then Rollo squatted down and had a good look at Ed's leg fastened to the axe haft. He shook his head over it and said things Ed couldn't understand. But a general sympathy seemed to emanate from him, and Ed found he was quickly losing the fear of death. Rollo, it seemed, was friendly. This appeared almost too good to be true.

Rollo left shortly after with a sort of mime which indicated he would come back, and Ed heard conversations with other men outside, and the noises of looting and hen-chasing and cursing. Then the voices withdrew, fading away into the distance until there was nothing save the sound of the wind in the hut roof and the trilling of curlews from the river.

Edmund was on his own.

Chapter 3

They came for him three days later.

By then Ed had given himself up for lost and lapsed into semi-consciousness. A terrible thirst burned his throat. Asser's body buzzed with flies and was beginning to give off a foul smell.

Ed knew there was no water nearer than Aulaf's hut, in the wooden tub that was kept by the door, and that was farther than he could have dragged himself. He had trusted in Rollo to come back, but Rollo had forsaken him. When he came for him at last Ed was on the edge of delirium and thought it was Oswy come to take him to Lundenburg.

After that it was worse, getting picked up and laid on a wooden sledge, and then the bumping and jolting and the men swearing around him... It seemed like a journey to eternity. And he knew he was going as a slave, to be mended, and then to serve, to get beaten like a dog. He knew all about slaves. Better that he had died, like Asser.

The men around him thought he wasn't worth their effort. He could sense their derision. But Rollo was their master's son and had to be obeyed, even though he was so young. They dragged Ed five miles to an old fort where they had decided to make a base. Ed knew the place: a collection of huts in a flat space surrounded by thick earth walls put up long ago, even before the Romans. All the inhabitants had fled, like his own folk. The land surrounding had been cleared and was well farmed, considering the poor ground – no doubt the reason the invaders had picked the spot. Ed knew there were deer to be found in the scrub, and hares. But none of it belonged to these arrogant sailors with their blond beards and crazy conversation! He groaned with rage and pain. What would Wistan have done?

The bed they put him on was clean and the roof above was better than Oswy's. Later a man came and cut the axe haft off his leg and Edmund felt his fingers exploring the dreadful pain and making it worse, until he passed out. But when he awoke the pain had gone and the same man brought him water and some meat broth of sorts, which tasted better than anything his mother had ever made. And then he slept.

He stayed in the hut for six weeks. When his leg was beginning to bear him again – and it was mending straight and well – they chained him to one of the roof posts, destroying his hope of escaping. The chain was put round his neck and secured with an iron bolt, and gave him some six strides of freedom – save he could not stride. He tried to tell himself it made no difference. He could not move after all. But it weighed on him heavier than a grinding-stone. It was a slave's badge indeed, putting him on the level of a dog.

Apart from that, he was not ill-treated. Rollo came to see him quite often and tried to talk to him. He sometimes drew on the earth floor with a stick to help communicate, and out of a natural curiosity they taught each other the prime words of their languages. Ed gathered that they wanted horses, they could do nothing without horses. Their own horses had not yet arrived. Ed did not know anyone rich enough to own a horse. He only knew peasants and farmers, and oxen did the work for them and sometimes the women.

Ed gathered that these invaders had come to settle, and the young men amongst them intended to join their leader Sven Forkbeard, who was presently devastating the north. They meant no harm (tell Asser that, Ed thought) but would take the things they wanted by force. There were older men and women amongst them who wanted to make a home and farm the land. Ed had seen women passing by his hut, and even two young girls not much older than himself. Rollo told him, with drawings, that there were two ships and seventy people, and messengers had been sent to find relations already here, in Essex, who would help them. Perhaps they would move on. Perhaps they would stay. "You will stay with me," Rollo assured Ed. But whether in chains, or of his own free will, Ed had no idea.

Ed had a very vague knowledge of what was happening in the country. There was nobody to bring news, living as they did out of the busy paths where messengers might pass by with tales of battles and invasions. He just knew enough to run if strange people with swords appeared on the shore. He had heard about battles of course, but who was fighting who, and why, he had little idea. It was something young men did, he had always thought. If you lost you became a slave. He was a slave already, and hadn't even fought yet.

Sitting chained to the roof post all day was incredibly boring, and not being able to see out was very frustrating. The man who watched over his leg told him with his fingers how many days before he could walk again, and Ed made marks with a stick on the floor and crossed them off every sundown.

Watching through the doorhole, he learned a good deal about the community just by their passing.

The leader of the expedition was a gnarled, grey-haired man called Ragnar. He gave orders quietly, was very active, and much respected. His oldest son, Ohtar, was the man who had killed Asser. He bossed people about in a louder and more aggressive fashion than his father, but when his father was there, he was quiet and attentive. Rollo, the younger son, was much in awe of Ohtar, whom he obviously hero-worshipped, but in his ways he was more like his father, quieter by nature, and not unkind.

Then there was the girl.

Estrid was Ragnar's daughter, twelve years old. She was very pretty with her long yellow hair fastened back with gold bands and eyes as bright as Rollo's. She was very quick and laughed a lot with the little brown girl (her maid?) who accompanied her. She had obviously been told not to go near Ed, but every time she passed her eyes looked his way. Ed would sit waiting for her, his ears alert for her funny, gurgling voice. She wore a turquoise tunic like Rollo's, but hers was pale and clean, and fastened with a beautiful silver brooch carved into a seahorse with jewelled eyes. Ed had never seen a girl so sweet and clean before. Perhaps, like Rollo, she would be attracted to him by his outstanding hair. With no action to fill his time, he dreamed about Estrid in a way new to him. There was no sickness in his body, the way his imagination ran riot.

The mother was a thin-faced, rather ill-looking woman with a sweet smile but not much energy. She, like her husband, was much respected and waited upon. Unlike his own mother, Edmund gathered that she was not expected to work hard. He wondered what sort of life they had left behind them, that they had been prepared to risk their lives across the German ocean. They were obviously rich and well respected and had a lot of people to serve them. From a land of rocks and ice, come south to find soft land and fertile soil and warm winters, they were in as strange a new life as he himself.

When there were still five marks on the floor uncrossed, and Ed was beginning to get excited about leaving the hut, he was astonished to have another prisoner thrust in alongside him and chained to the same post.

This was a boy of roughly his own age, extremely muddy and ill-clad. He had brown curly hair and brown eyes and a dirt-brown face and was in a fighting mood. The man that brought him in beat him quite savagely about the head until he fell down crying, and Ed was left to find it in himself to say a few words of comfort. In truth, he felt a little dubious about his new companion. So long had he held sway as the only – rather well-looked-after – prisoner that he wasn't sure he wanted his position usurped.

"Shut up. You're not hurt," he said.

"I am!" (fiercely). Then, after some more sniffing: "They've taken my pony, Aurelia. They've stolen her! And when I tried to beat them off they chased me away. But I followed them, to get her back, and they – they laughed, and wouldn't give her back to me. I wouldn't leave her. I followed them and now look what's happened."

"Lucky they didn't kill you. What are you complaining for?"

"I wasn't doing them any harm!"

Ed didn't feel disposed to argue. He wasn't sure how to take this boy. He seemed to have behaved like an idiot and got all he deserved. Following them back ... when he could have run for it!

"They want horses. They'll take whatever they find."

"She's too small."

"They aren't cruel to animals. They love horses." He had gathered this from Rollo's attitude, and seen for himself that the cows and pigs they had rounded up were well tended. He threw it out for comfort. He didn't know about horses, but there was a cow, Wulfwyn, he had once thought fondly of and he remembered crying when she died calving. And Oswy's dog...

After a while, in the dusk, the boy calmed down and they talked. Ed told the boy what had happened to him, and what he knew of the community they had both landed in. The boy told him his name was Sigewulf and he lived with his grandparents who had a little fishing boat on the estuary to the south, a few miles away. He had been collecting cooking wood, loading it on to his pony, when the strangers suddenly appeared. They were hunting hares, not very successfully, and found their new prey far more fun.

"If you kick and fight, you can't win." Ed told him what had happened to Asser. "The big one, Ohtar, is really tough. Otherwise, they're all right."

"It was Ohtar who would not let me go."

Sigy – as Edmund soon called him – asked what was going to happen to them.

Ed had given this matter a good deal of thought during his long hours chained to the post. He assumed that, when he was unchained, he was to be Rollo's servant (a better word than slave). His dream was to run away and find his family, but he knew that it would be impossible. They would have a way of stopping him, even without the chain. He tried to convince himself – being an optimist by nature – that life even as a slave could possibly be better in this Norsemen's camp than with his family. His family was now homeless, without land, without hope. Oswy was a pain, and made him work like a slave anyway. Without Wistan, home meant little. If he was homesick, what was he homesick for? For this was his home. He had no other. He knew the place. He knew the terrain, the tides, the shore, the hunting and fishing, better than his masters. And, being practical, his prisoner's food was far better than any his mother had concocted, and the huts the men had constructed were stouter than any Oswy and his father had managed to put up. The lower orders – whether they were slaves or not Edmund could not tell – were cheerful and well fed, and there was more laughing than lamenting.

Besides, to be with the Norsemen was to be on the winning side. Edmund was not so stupid that he could not see the advantage of that. Their king Sven Forkbeard was cutting swathes through the north and looking set to take the whole country. Forkbeard also had a brilliant young son called Cnut to help him. The English king had a son too, with the same name as Edmund, and there was word that he was a much finer soldier than his father, but so far he hadn't achieved much.

Oswy had always talked longingly of going to fight, and Ed knew that he in his turn wanted to go and be a soldier. But if he stayed, and it came to fighting, whose side would he be on then? Serving Rollo, he would be fighting against his own brothers. He couldn't do that!

"When they unchain us, we can escape on Aurelia," Sigy said. "She's very fast."

Edmund laughed out loud at this. What was the good of making plans?

The man who looked after his leg came in the evening with Rollo and told Rollo that Ed was now ready to work.

"Tomorrow he can be let free." He crossed off Edmund's marks on the floor, leaving only one.

"In the morning, you work."

"And this one?" Rollo pointed at Sigy.

The man shrugged. "If he doesn't run away – "

"He can look after his pony, and the horses when they come."

So far there had been no opposition to this new encampment. This was because Essex was largely held by the Norsemen, and the Saxon people had learned to keep their heads down and live with them. The last big clash had been at Maldon over twenty years ago, when the great Byrhtnoth had been defeated and killed by the Danish invaders. That was where Edmund's father had got his crack on the head which had so enfeebled him. At least, unlike Byrhtnoth, he still had his head – Byrhtnoth's had been cut off and carried away as a trophy, and the great warrior was buried without it.

"I'm not going to stay," Sigy said. "As soon as I get the chance I'll be gone."

When the morning came and his chain was taken off, Edmund felt an excitement going out into the daylight that had him trembling. The doctor, Sigurd, made him walk up and down, trying out his leg. When he was satisfied he fetched Ragnar and they spoke together. The headman of the slaves, Thored, was called. And Rollo. They looked him over as if he were an ox at market. Thored nodded. He took Ed by the arm and led him away to where the big fire burned in the middle of the compound. Various pots bubbled in the embers, sending out tantalizing aromas of food, and several of the women slaves were working there, handling the pots with hardened hands.

Thored called to another slave and he came running, carrying a branding iron, which he thrust into the fire. Ed guessed what it was, and tried not to believe it. But he knew slaves were branded. It was a fact of life. He made himself remember Wistan, and his face as he walked on the fire, proud and unflinching. Thored held his arm in a grip of iron. Ed lifted his chin, and hoped Thored would not hear the pounding of his heart. The slave lifted out the now smoking iron, and pulled Ed's tattered clothes away to bare his back. Out of the corner of his eye Ed saw Estrid and her maid watching, holding each other's hands. Everyone was watching.

The smell was disgusting, and the sound of sizzling flesh. Ed pretended the pain wasn't there, like Wistan, but could feel his proud look collapsing as the fire bit. But he did not move, or stagger, or make a sound. The burn screamed in his flesh, and Ed looked beyond all the watchers into the sky, to keep his head up, and fastened his gaze on two gliding gulls. The weather was fine and the sky cloudless. The gulls swooped and their cries sounded to Ed like the wails he might so easily have let rip, if he hadn't had Wistan's example to hold him together.

Thored obviously approved of his behaviour, for he smiled and said something in a kind voice. His grip eased, and he took Ed back to Ragnar and Rollo with a hand on his shoulder. Ohtar had joined his father. He had his beautiful sword bared in his hand. He gave it to his father, who held it out in front of Ed.

"Swear by your God. Your Christus," Ragnar commanded. "To serve me." He spoke in English. "Your Christ. Christus," he repeated, to make sure Edmund got the message.

Edmund laid his hand on the sword and swore.

To him, it was like being chained again. The words were a whisper, but bound like the chain.

Ohtar, having no sense of honour, said

brutally, "If you try to escape, you will be hunted and your hands cut off. If we cannot find you, we will kill your friend Sigy instead."

Ed found he was shivering, in spite of the sun.

The sword blade flashed as Ohtar thrust it back in its scabbard.

Ed watched it, longing to hold such a weapon, to hold the power that was now turned against him. With his hand on the sword, taking the oath, he felt that his own Christ, if he loved him, would give him the same power one day. He was deeply moved, humiliated by becoming a slave, yet at the same time excited by the turn his life had taken. He felt strong, almost as if touching the sword had given him a semblance of its power.

Yes, he would serve these invaders. Until the time came...

Chapter 4

Rollo said, "You can come down to the shore with me. I have to check that the ship is safe – that's my job. Every day."

Rollo wasn't quite sure what to do with a slave now he had one. At first he spoke in a bossy manner, but quite soon he slipped into being friendly. Ed replied in kind. He wasn't used to being a slave, after all. If Rollo wasn't going to teach him, he would be himself.

The place Ragnar had chosen for his new home was on an undulating piece of open ground used in the past as common grazing. It had been fortified long before the Romans came by the digging of earth banks all round it, and there was a steep knoll on the northern side which must have been built as a watch-tower, for from the top one could command a view to the north of the wide river mouth meeting the German ocean.

Ragnar's men had thrown up an impressive settlement, with a longhouse for living in and several huts for stores. While he had been chained up Ed had been aware of the work being carried out around him, but until now had no idea of its extent. No Saxons he knew had ever built so fast and so strongly as these fair-haired foreigners.

To be out in the open was like being reborn. The hut he had been held in was, like all their dwellings, windowless and sunk into a pit in the ground. Snug enough – although smoky – in the winter, in summer it was dank, dark and depressing.

The two boys set off, out of the camp. If this was being a slave, walking in the sunshine along the trodden track towards the river, Ed did not think it too terrible. Even the raging pain of the burn on his back and the aching of his feeble leg muscles could not quench his spirits, which soared like the seabirds into the air. Rollo, unlike Ohtar, posed no threat. He talked without ceasing. Ed had learned to pick up – generally – the gist of what he was saying, but on this soft summer day a lot of it went past like the breeze beneath the gull's wing. He was so actively happy to be back on his shore, alive, out of the darkness.

They came down to the water, scrambling

over the banks of sea-lavender and thrift, and Ed saw the longship lying at anchor, her bow just grounding on the mud. Quite close now, her size astonished him. The longhouse would have fitted inside her. Eighty feet in length, she was built of long planks curved up at stem and stern to give a massive and frightening appearance. So wide inside, Ed could see that stalls could be built to carry livestock, and bulky stores carried, still leaving room for the rowers to man the oars on either side.

Rollo kept talking about the horses coming from home, which now made sense. Until he had set eyes on this boat, Ed couldn't imagine what Rollo meant. He had never seen a boat you could put horses in. Not until now. Rollo said they trained their horses to load into a ship. First they put in old quiet mares who knew all about it, and the young horses went in after them and learned not to be frightened.

When the horses came, Ohtar and his friends were going off to join Sven Forkbeard.

"I want to go too, but my father says I am too young," Rollo said. He made a face, obviously disagreeing.

Now he was a slave, Ed didn't see how he could become a soldier. Maybe it was a good thing. The stories he had heard of the Battle of Maldon and Byrhtnoth's killing had been horrific. He thought of the weight of Ohtar's sword coming down in anger – it would cut a person clean in two! His own brothers hadn't had a sword between them, only iron knives they had sharpened on their father's stone, and a homemade spear apiece. They had marched off when the King's men had come calling, full of spirits. But Sven Forkbeard's men were highly trained soldiers, not farm boys. Many were mercenaries from far-distant countries, even dark-skinned men from Africa, who killed for money. Ed had heard plenty of stories. But seen nothing.

Rollo's words stirred him, but to bitterness. First a peasant – and now not even that. A slave.

"They say your king's son, Edmund – like you – is a good soldier. And Sven Forkbeard's son, Cnut, is a brilliant warrior ... we sailed with his ships. Ohtar wants to serve Cnut."

Rollo skimmed stones over the water, still talking. Ed saw that he was a boy without spite or arrogance, not disposed to play the master, and soon he was skimming stones too. They competed to skim the farthest, but they were equally matched, and soon gave up and emptied the fish-traps instead. The tide was receding but still fairly high, so there were not many fish to gather. Rollo killed them with stones as ably as Ed, and they carried them home and gave them to the women.

As Rollo obviously didn't quite know what to do with a slave, Thored put Edmund to work later milking the cows. They had collected a dozen or so and made a compound for them. Sigy's pony Aurelia was tethered beside them, a funny little thing with hairy legs and a great deal of mane and tail. Under her forelock bright eyes glittered. She had sweat marks over her back – she had been used all day for carting firewood. Sigy was still chained up. Ed was now allocated a bed in the longhouse in the servants' end, in the farthest corner. Rollo and his family slept at the other end, on raised benches covered with clean woollen rugs. Ed had straw on the floor and a mothy sheepskin, much as he was used to.

When he had finished milking and eaten his supper of hare stew and bread, he was given a plateful to take to Sigy. Sigy was really pleased to see him.

"I didn't expect to see you again. I thought you'd run away."

"I can't." Ed explained the solemn swearing on the sword.

Sigy was scornful. "That's only words! They won't keep me. Once the chain is off –"

"It's not words. It's my honour."

"Pooh," said Sigy.

Ed realized that Sigy was an ignorant peasant. He didn't understand the simplest things. Ed's father had been a warrior, and taught his children the behaviour of the lords and councillors who commanded the warriors. If Sigy hadn't heard of honour ... well, it was to be expected of a poor fisherboy.

Ed told Sigy all he had found out – that Ohtar and the young men were going away to fight as soon as their horses came. He told him about Sven Forkbeard's son Cnut arriving with his ships.

"If I am free I shall fight Sven Forkbeard and his son! I shan't be a slave," Sigy declared. "I shall run away to be a soldier."

Edmund was scornful.

"You! You've no sword, no spear. They'll laugh at you."

"If you're Rollo's slave, are you going to help him fight on the side of Sven and Cnut?"

This question silenced Edmund. How could he, against his own king? It wasn't possible.

"Rollo is too young to fight," he said. "It won't happen."

"He won't be too young always."

For all Sigy was ignorant, he knew how to

make disturbing remarks.

"Will you sleep with me here tonight?"

"No. I've been given a place in the long-house."

Ed then saw that Sigy was lonely and probably frightened. His dirty face was tracked with tear-marks. He squatted down on the floor beside him and said, "Perhaps they will let you free tomorrow. The work isn't hard and the food's good. You can say you will help with the cows."

But Sigy started to cry again and said he wanted his granny.

In the evening Edmund walked across to the knoll that had been built as a watch-tower, and scrambled on to the top of it. It was just turning dusk and the distant water was orange with the last glow of the sun. It was very still, and the smoke of the cooking fires drifted from the roof of the longhouse and softly streaked the dusk-violet sky. A few stars were out, and the familiar smell of seawrack and mud and trampled grass, mixed with the wood-smoke, made Ed suddenly blink back tears of homesickness – for his mother and Oswy and the old life by the shore, for his companions and his father and the old men who made the decisions. What if they had stayed? Would the men have been killed like Asser, or would they all have been taken as slaves? There were too many of them. They might well have been left in peace, to get on with their lives.

What has happened to me, Ed wondered. He didn't belong anywhere. He was crying like Sigy. Wistan! The memory of his brother wrenched him.

A sharp voice hailed him.

He turned round and saw Ohtar standing below him. He knew Ohtar thought he was thinking of running away. He came down to meet him, and Ohtar growled something at him. Ohtar's eyes were like chips of bright glass. He was evil, Ed thought, brutal. He hit Ed round the head so that his brain spun and pushed him in the direction of the longhouse. His voice lashed him, like hot water spitting on a rock. But Ed did not know what he said. He only knew that Ohtar, to whom he had sworn loyalty, wasn't worth the sacrifice of his freedom. Ragnar and Rollo perhaps, and some of the others, but not Ohtar.

He hated Ohtar.

Chapter 5

A messenger came to say that Ragnar's horses had arrived on the shore of the Thames, at Beamfleot, and were awaiting collection. Ohtar and his fellow warriors were excited and relieved, and set off with a body of servants to collect them. Rollo went with them, but Ed was not allowed to go. Ragnar said he was more use at home.

"Unchain the little one. We can set him to work too."

So Sigy was unchained, and reunited with his pony Aurelia. Even Ed was impressed at how the pony whinnied when she saw him and pulled at her tether to meet him. Sigy flung his thin arms round her neck and rained kisses into her mane. He was given the job of collecting firewood, one of the most tedious of the chores. And a bed next to Edmund.

"I am going to run away," he whispered to Ed in the night.

Ohtar was not there to make him swear an oath to obey. But with his belly full of deer meat and beans, Sigy added, "Tomorrow."

"You're a fool," Ed said. But not with any conviction.

The camp was quiet without the young men. The women were more in evidence, going about their jobs in an organized and intelligent way which Ed found striking. They were no peasants, like the people he came from. Ragnar was obviously a man of standing, what they called a jarl, and he and his lady ordered the work, from the clearing and tilling of land to the spinning and weaving of cloth. Ragnar seemed to be enormously rich – no doubt from earlier visits to pillage and demand ransoms – and sent men away to buy all the things they needed. Neither Sigy nor Ed had come across such a way of life before, never having rubbed shoulders with kings and earls.

"You could do worse than work for a man like him," Ed said to Sigy.

They lay squashed together in their corner of the longhouse, surrounded by snoring slaves. The big fire glowed in the centre of the floor and Ragnar and some of the older men were still sitting there, drinking and talking. It was late, yet scarcely dark. The smell of woodsmoke mingled with the smell of the summer night over the marshes.

Sigy said suddenly, "I'm going back to my granny."

"Stay here. If they catch you they will punish you and chain you up again."

"I'm no use to them chained up."

In the far end of the longhouse, slipping through the shadows, Ed thought he saw the girl Estrid. Although he was a slave, she smiled at him when he was with Rollo. Ed thought he was in love, because every time he saw her he felt the colour flame in his face. Or did she smile at him merely for the colour of his hair? Even the old women smiled at him for the colour of his hair. They called him Firehead, just as his own people had.

He belonged nowhere.

One day, he thought, I shall find my place. I will not stay a slave for ever. But for now, I am waiting. He had a dream, of being heroic and claiming Estrid from a grateful Ragnar. Estrid was always laughing in his dream. God knew, he had nothing but his dreams.

The next day it rained. Ed and Sigy were put to enlarging a drainage ditch to keep the water from the cattle pen. Wielding a couple of inadequate spades, they slithered about in mud all day, getting shouted at whenever they stopped. Ed did not like it, but he was used to doing jobs he didn't like, shouted at by Oswy. What was the difference? But Sigy said he'd had enough.

"At supper, when everyone's eating, I shall take Aurelia and go."

The dogs wouldn't bark, as they would if he went in the middle of the night. They would think he was just going about his chores. The dogs got their bones at supper time, and this kept them mightily occupied.

Ed thought Sigy was a spoiled brat. No doubt his granny spoiled him abominably. He wasn't used to hard work – he didn't even have to walk far with Aurelia to carry him.

"Don't go," he said.

But Sigy wouldn't listen.

The rain stopped and the sun came out just as it was sinking, a flaming apology for the horrid day. The soaked timbers of the new buildings gave off a strong smell of sap, almost steaming, and the glistening mud threw back the brightness of the sunset.

Ed went to the door of the longhouse with Sigy, and stopped.

Sigy crossed over to the animal pen and fetched Aurelia out. Outside the bare field of the encampment the thick brush and straggling woods closed in, cut only by the wide path that went out from the gateway to join the old Roman road from Othona. On the other side reeds and marsh ran away to the northern river. But Sigy needed to go south, where his home was.

No one saw him as he vaulted on to Aurelia and turned her head towards the gateway. Pressing his heels to her side, he cantered away. . .

Ed stood dumbly, his instinct wanting to run after him, his brain telling him to stay. The sun flared in the west, sinking behind the trees, and in its flaming light there was suddenly a great swirling movement – horses, riders, shouting and singing. A crowd of men on horses was silhouetted, trotting down the wide ride towards the gate of the settlement.

Sigy had nowhere to go. His little pony, astonished by the party advancing towards her, slithered to a halt and, before Sigy could think what to do, Ohtar on his horse galloped out of the throng and tore the reins from Sigy's hands. Aurelia spun round and was dragged back into the camp alongside Ohtar, her rider petrified with fear at the sudden end of his escape.

At the sound of hooves and the shouting of

greetings, everyone poured out of the long-house. Laughing, Ohtar swung down from his horse, pulled Sigy off his pony and in one quick movement unsheathed his sword and slashed at the hand he held. Sigy fell away, screaming, and Ohtar tossed the severed hand to his favourite dog. Another dog ran up, leaping up for favours, and Ohtar grabbed Sigy again. His sword blade flashed in the sun as he raised it.

"*No!*"

Ed flung himself at Ohtar with such force that the sword flew out of his hand. He was berserk with hate, so that he sent Ohtar reeling. Ohtar slipped in the mud and went over backwards. Ed kicked him savagely in the head, wanting to put out the light that glittered in the furious eyes, but rough hands pulled him back and his arms were twisted up behind his back so forcefully that he cried out.

"Enough!"

Ragnar was suddenly there, his wife close behind him. He shouted something at Ohtar, and Ohtar was on his feet. His face was crimson with anger but he dared not cross his father.

Ed was too blind with pain for Sigy to take in much of what was happening. Ragnar was angry with Ohtar but only fleetingly, and it seemed a general opinion that Sigy hadn't deserved to lose both hands, but one was reasonable enough for the offence. Sigurd the doctor picked Sigy up bodily and carried him quickly away, trailing a river of bright blood, and Ed had a glimpse of Estrid's white and anguished face before he too was manhandled away.

Ohtar came with him.

They took him to his old hut and tied him by the wrists to the two roof posts. Then his tunic was torn apart across his back, Ohtar's servant was sent for some birch branches and he was beaten until he lost consciousness. When he came to he was beaten again. And then again. Three times.

Then he was chained back to his old post and left for the night.

Chapter 6

Through their terrible punishments, a bond was formed between Edmund and Sigy that was never to be broken.

Sigy did not mention his granny again. Ed knew that he thought he would be useless to the old people with only one hand. Slicing off his hand had sliced off his past. He grew up overnight. They were chained together in their old hut until they were fit for work again. They wept, slept, talked and strengthened together. Ohtar came and swore at them, and said that if Sigy tried to escape again, he would cut off Ed's hand and, if Ed tried to escape, Sigy would lose his other hand. If they escaped together, they would be hunted down and killed.

"We'll kill *him*!" Sigy hissed.

"He's going away to fight. With luck he'll get killed by someone else."

Wistan perhaps.

Hated as Ohtar was, he was the son of Ragnar who was a wise and sympathetic leader. Rollo came to the hut when no one was about and said that his mother and father were angry at what Ohtar had done and his father had spoken sternly to him. But it was recognized that Ohtar was the strength of the family, and it was common for slaves to be treated as they had been treated. Rollo did not seem to think that Ohtar had acted harshly. And, even with his little experience of life beyond the seashore, Ed knew from hearsay that such punishments were common. He had been beaten enough by his own father, after all. But not like Ohtar had beaten him. It was three days before he could stand again.

Sigurd came to them every day, to dress Sigy's stump. Sigy seemed more upset about a dog having eaten his hand, than actually losing it.

Ed thought this very funny. "It's a hand-fed dog," he said wittily. Sigy hit him across the back where it hurt and they fought, rolling over and over in the dirt until their pain stopped them.

One day Sigurd brought Estrid with him. She had a tunic over her arm made of grey wool which she gave to Ed. It wasn't new, but with it was a braided belt of many colours, with gold threads woven into it and neat little tassels at each end. She said something, by which Ed understood she had made it herself. Her cheeks went bright pink as she gave it to him, and Ed's own feelings were aroused when he saw her colour, and he felt the same flush burning his own face. He was overcome, and had to turn away. Fine he would look with a red face to clash with his orange hair! Never having seen himself in a mirror, only a reflection in water, he had no idea of the effect of his riotous fiery curls, white skin and golden-green eyes on the feelings of a lonely twelve-year-old girl. Estrid could expect to be married within a year or two and, having decided to give her heart to a slave, she was not at that time expecting a happy future. She would marry whom her father chose, probably a much older warrior with land and riches won from the Saxons. She was attractive and desirable and was already being approached by friends of her father for their favourite son. But her heart went where it willed and she could do nothing to help it. The slave boy with the glorious hair was where it had landed.

Later, when Ed was lying prone with the belt in his hands, he felt a hard little knob in one end, just above the tassel, and when he examined it he found a tiny solid gold heart set in the thickness of the braid, harnessed tight with a gold thread. He stared at it for a long time, but said nothing to Sigy. From that moment, he felt no bitterness at what had happened to him.

Outside, with the coming of the horses, all was abustle with preparations for the young warriors to depart, to meet up with their leader Sven Forkbeard. Sven had fought his way south and was now somewhere in the vicinity of Oxford, moving towards Lundenburg.

In ten days' time, having rested their travel-weary horses, Ohtar and his band of companions left the camp.

Edmund and Sigy watched them go with feelings of relief. They were geared up in chainmail and helmets and carried shields, swords and spears, and had outriders with banners to make a fearsome convoy on the road. No doubt they would get provisions by force and make a rapid journey. The horses were stocky animals from Scandinavia, mostly pale in colour, with short backs and legs and long flowing manes and tails. The men's legs dangled down by the horses' knees, but Sigy said he had never seen horses so large. In Britain most of the horses were strong and stocky, but lacking in height. Men were used to riding with their feet near the ground.

Feeling as if a great cloud had lifted from the camp, Ed and Sigy ventured out into the air. All was quiet on the soft autumn morning, the women going about their work, the older men directing the slaves, the cows going out to pasture. Ed and Sigy were given light duties herding, and recovered their spirits moving across the marshes with the grazing animals. Gauzy clouds drifted high in the almost colourless sky, and the sea sparkled on the horizon. Ed, sitting on the saltings looking out at the white shore and the soft lifting of the waves, thought of the tumult of fighting that Ohtar and his friends had gone to meet. Were his brothers there, he wondered. Wistan and Godric had now been three years away. They would be twenty and nineteen now, grown men. Or rotting bodies, skeletons even. Not Wistan! Ed prayed.

Ed understood why they had gone. What was there on this remote shore to engage a young man's ambition? If Ohtar and Rollo hadn't taken him, he would by now have set off to fight Sven Forkbeard himself, young as he was. Or so he told himself. A young man wanted more than seeing to the cows.

But now he was bound by more than

respect of his parents' wishes. He was bound by honour to Ragnar, by the love of Estrid and, most of all, by his relationship with Sigy. Sigy now depended on him, unable to cut his own meat, milk a cow, bridle a horse, fasten his tunic, make fire. Sigy was in a sense shackled to him by his terrible wound. For now. But now would not last for ever.

Ed lay back on the peaty hummock he had chosen for a seat, watching the swooping of the gulls overhead as they chased one of their flock with a fish in its mouth. He wished he had his catapult – something else denied to Sigy. Shooting down gulls was fun. (But they were horrid to eat.) The raucous cries echoed along the empty shore. Since the invaders had come, nobody poached upon their presence. Everyone had withdrawn, even the priest from the ancient church on the old Roman wall. No doubt he would be back when he saw how the land lay, calling to see if Ragnar was a Christian or a heathen. Ed was a Christian – or so his mother had told him. It paid. No doubt Ragnar would see it that way too. Sven was spectacularly heathen, acting in a very heathenish way from all the evidence. Lucky it had been Ragnar and not Sven who had landed in their quiet corner.

Something sharp dug into Ed's neck.

He wriggled away and found a more comfortable spot, then idly put his hand up to find the stone or whatever it was. His fingers explored something uncomfortably sharp.

"Sigy!"

Ed wriggled over and scrabbled under the roots of the sea-lavender. Sigy wandered over.

"What is it?"

It was a spearhead. Ed pulled it out and laid it reverently on the sand. He looked back into the hole and found four more. They had been tied around with a length of linen and a piece of cord which was now shredded and rotten. Once good linen . . . still beautiful spearheads. They were long and narrow and vicious and had a pattern of leaves incised on the flatter part of the blades. Ed knew a good spear when he saw one.

"Treasure!"

"However did they come there?"

"Someone hid them. Look how they're wrapped. I bet he meant to come back for them one day. They're beauties."

Even Ohtar could not boast better spears than these. Ed remembered the weapons fastened to his horse, freshly sharpened and polished, and the beautiful sword which had so deftly severed Sigy's hand. It had a hilt inlaid with silver in the shape of a serpent, with yellow topaz eyes. It was the most desirable thing Edmund had ever seen. The only weapon he had ever possessed had been a home-made spear fashioned from an old spade which Oswy had made him. It would not even kill a rat. But these spears – they were a rich man's spears, perhaps a Roman's, from the old fort. His eyes widened, alive with pleasure.

"What a find! One day we'll use these, Sigy, eh?"

"Who on? Ohtar?"

"Perhaps."

Since Ohtar's cruelty towards Sigy Ed did not feel as bound by his oath as before. To Ragnar, perhaps – a good man – even to Rollo, and certainly to Estrid – he would never betray them. But Ohtar... Ohtar did not deserve his loyalty.

"How can we keep them?" Sigy asked. He reached for one, turning it over in his hand. Ed caressed them with both hands. He still found it hard to accept Sigy's livid stump, striped with the marks of Sigurd's rough sewing. And he felt for Sigy when he watched how he attempted all the simple things he had once done with both hands, working out ways, using his teeth, even a foot. He was stubborn and persistent, and he had never once complained – only breathed his hatred for Ohtar.

"I still have my spear hand," he said.

"Yes. You will make use of these one day. We'll keep them hidden here, back in the same hole, until we need them."

And Ed wrapped the spearheads carefully again in the remnants of their old binding and put them back in the hole. They marked the hole with stones and took a bearing of its position from a clump of gnarled thicket and the remains of an old Roman jetty.

Ed felt in his bones that one day they would need them, Sigy and he. There was no way they could be slaves for ever.

Chapter 7

Four years later Ohtar came home, full of tales of glory. Sven Forkbeard had died tamely in his bed and his young blond son Cnut now led the invaders' army. Ohtar would follow him to the ends of the earth. As they feasted round the glowing central hearth, Ed and Sigy strained their ears to pick up the story. The English King Aethelred had died. His son Edmund was fighting for his crown and Cnut was fighting to take it from him. It seemed they were equally matched and after several battles their armies were becoming exhausted.

Ohtar had come home to gather together reinforcements. Word went round the slave bench that he had spoken of taking the strongest slaves.

Edmund lay watching the leaping flames and the smoke hanging in the high roof. The specially-killed ox hung in shreds from the spit. They had all eaten well, the slaves too, and Ohtar was still cutting hunks from the haunch, using his sword as if to boast his standing – the beautiful sword with its silver serpent and topaz eyes. How many men had it killed? Ed felt his heart throbbing with a rare excitement, watching the silver blade flash red above the flames. The sword that had killed Asser, and severed Sigy's hand ... how long ago it seemed now! Ed thought, if he doesn't take us, we will go.

As if reading his thoughts, Sigy said bitterly, "He won't take me."

"He will. If I go, you come too."

"To fight our own people?"

"To get away," Edmund said. "When it comes to battle, we can choose. We will be free men."

If the strongest slaves were to go, they would be chosen. They were fifteen – Sigy fourteen – tall and strong and straight, forged by hard work and a hard life. Even with only one hand Sigy could do a man's work. They could sleep out without shelter, walk all day without food, carry the heaviest load. The thought of leaving was like the brightest spark in the fire, glowing in Ed's imagination. Save for one thing ... like a dash of ice the realization... His eyes sought, as they always did, the figure of Estrid far away on the girls' bench. To leave Estrid would be to leave part of himself behind.

Their love affair was very strange. Giving no explanation, she had refused to look at any of the suitors brought to meet her by her parents. She said she was not ready. She wanted only Edmund, although she dared not say it. Her mother suspected it, her little brown maid Hilde knew. Several of the young girls knew, and giggled, and made eyes at Ed and Sigy Onehand themselves. But they knew better than to approach Ed when Estrid had laid claim to him. Of course they were kept apart, but their paths inevitably crossed and there were more giggles and hands meeting, a brushing kiss sometimes. They were beaten if they were suspected. Ed had been beaten three times, unjustly in his view, for he wasn't interested in any girl save Estrid, and Estrid he had only spoken to four times. Once he had touched her hand. He knew she loved him as he loved her. The little gold heart swung from his belt and gnawed at his thigh when he lay asleep. He knew she watched him; he could feel her eyes on him, like a caress from the end of the hall. She had grown more beautiful with every passing year, and was now sixteen, tall and straight and white as a lily. Perhaps because their love was hopeless, it flourished like the bold lily itself.

Sigy knew too. He laughed, but kindly.

"A man would stand a chance with Hilde. But Estrid! You're mad."

But now perhaps there was a chance to get away, to throw off his slavery and gain standing and honour in battle. He could come back as a hero like Ohtar and ask for Estrid's hand. What a dream!

But he wasn't a Dane, a Norseman. He was Anglo-Saxon, half Celt. The Saxons had come from lands by the Baltic Sea, the Celts from Eastern Europe. Ed knew no geography, but he knew the hotch-potch nature of his people, recognized a Roman nose when he saw one, and the colouring of the Scandinavian invaders. Sigy boasted of being descended from the wild queen Boudicca – his granny had told him. Ed laughed at this and even Sigy found it funny. His pony was called Aurelia after his granny's friend who boasted she was pure Roman. Pure! Nobody was pure Roman any more. Not after five hundred years!

So who was he fighting? It was a riddle and not to be resolved easily. For now, getting away was what mattered. Once on the march, anything could happen.

Sigy was terrified he would be rejected.

"Thored will tell him you can work as well as anyone," Ed said. "I've not noticed you getting off jobs because of your hand!"

"No. Because you're always with me," Sigy said in a low voice.

They had never been separated, and now could not imagine it. There were plenty of other slaves who spoke the same language, some much the same age, but neither Ed nor Sigy had looked for other companionship. They were rarely given tasks apart, as if it were acknowledged that they worked better as a pair, and the few things Sigy could not do were automatically done by Ed without a word being said.

Sigy asked Thored if it was true they might be joining Ohtar's band of warriors.

"If you're unlucky, yes. The fighting is very close. Cnut is only across the water and Ohtar has promised him a band of men. The fighting has been so fierce that both armies sorely need fresh souls." He laughed. "Are you volunteering?"

"Yes!"

"You're mad."

"Sigy too. If Ohtar thinks he cannot serve, please put a word in for him."

Thored shrugged. "Ohtar will choose."

Most of the slaves were uneducated

peasants, old enough to have more sense than Ed. Not many were keen to go, recognizing a good berth when they saw it. Ragnar's rule was not harsh, and the older men were paid off and freed eventually, when their worth was used up. But Ed could not wait that long.

Then the word came he was chosen, along with Sigy and twelve others, all the strongest and most active. He knew Rollo had pleaded for him. Ohtar did not care if they were killed and was happy enough to take them. They were given new tunics and cloaks, and leather helmets and shoes, but no weapons. Not until battle was to be joined. Ed thought of the precious spears, and determined to fetch a couple before they marched. Then if they fell out of the party, they would be armed.

The boys, so eager to go, did not heed the murmurings that spread around the benches. Ohtar's weary companions were questioning what use untrained slave boys would be to the remains of Cnut's mercenaries, but Ohtar said force of numbers meant everything.

"They will fight well enough when Iron-sides' men come at them! It's called self-preservation. What else have we got? We give everything in our power. This is all I have, and I give it willingly."

In the last battle between the two armies Cnut had been defeated. He was now said to be retreating to his ships on the Thames. Edmund Ironsides was in pursuit.

"His ships on the Thames – it's so close, Sigy!" Ed whispered. "Only a day's march!"

Stories of fighting, plundering, torching and looting had been bandied about as long as Ed could remember, but never had the action come near to him. The settlement was uneasy, the cattle gathered in, watchmen sent up to the hill to the south. Ohtar, having rested three days, was ready to join Cnut again with his new homespun force. There were only twelve of his companions left from the original twenty.

Right up to the last moment Ragnar would not give Rollo permission to go, although the boy was desperate to join his brother. Ragnar, growing old, had already lost two sons in raiding England, and was likely now to lose Ohtar. He wanted his youngest to stay out of danger. But even he could see it was a lost cause. At fifteen Rollo was strong and brave and, unlike the slaves, had been well trained in sword handling and killing. He had his own helmet of bronze and a mail coat like Ohtar, and a sword nearly as fine as Ohtar's, and Ohtar wanted him at his side. Unlike the motley crew of slaves, Rollo was an impressive addition to his band and would please Cnut.

It was only on the afternoon of the day before they were to leave that Ragnar granted his permission. Ohtar laughed as Rollo capered with joy, but Ragnar's eyes were full of tears.

"Edmund will attend you on the expedition. He is a good boy. Send for him to make your preparations."

Although Ed had been singled out long ago as Rollo's personal slave, Rollo was an independent boy and had made little use of Ed save for looking after his horse. They got on well together and would have had much in common if it hadn't been for the gulf between them. Rollo lived in the household end of the longhouse at the far end from the slaves and Ed had rarely entered this private area. It was partitioned off and had curtains hanging across the entrance.

When he was sent for, he hesitated at the curtain.

As he did so, it was pulled aside by Estrid. She was as surprised as Ed and they both stared at each other, colouring up. Estrid looked as if she had been crying.

She said suddenly, violently, "Please come

back! I can't bear it if I never see you again! My father will free you, I promise!"

Ed had scarcely ever been so close to her, let alone heard words that swamped his senses with such sudden excitement. It was all he could do not to take her and cover her face with kisses. But with the great curtain caught back he could see Ohtar over her shoulder, glancing up, and Rollo talking to Ragnar. The mother was there too. He was only a slave. He had to step back as she – realizing the danger – walked on. Tears poured down her cheeks.

Ed was so shaken he couldn't move for a moment. Then he saw Ohtar's expression, which galvanized him back to life. Had he seen? His face was like a thundercloud. He said something to his mother and gestured towards Ed, but the mother shook her head and said something softly, sadly. Ohtar said something roughly, but now she answered sharply, imperiously, putting him down, and Ohtar glowered and said no more.

All this was quite missed by Rollo, who was now throwing open his wooden chest to pull out his belongings. Ragnar stood by him, smiling at his excitement. Ragnar too had fought at fifteen, making his first journey to England to run riot across the Lincolnshire fens, killing, and firing villages. He could still remember the bloody excitement of it, mixed with shame at seeing the bodies of children and old women, and the shame drowned in great draughts of stolen mead as they sat drinking round the victorious bonfires, the hot sparks flying into the night. How could he deny the same thrill to his dear Rollo? Rollo would have years to grow old in, improving the settlement. With luck, after the fighting he would be rewarded with land and riches, or find his own plunder. There was no other way to become wealthy in these haphazard times.

Ragnar, dreaming of old times, was not aware of the charged atmosphere that came with Ed's appearance. He recognized Ohtar's bad temper – Ohtar was far from being his favourite son – but he found it hard these days to overrule him. His own ways, away from battle, had become more gentle, and Ohtar by contrast had grown proud and overbearing. Success in battle had encouraged the worst in his nature, his cruelty and conceit. But by such power, these days, a man survived.

Ed helped Rollo pack his belongings into as small a parcel as possible, and laid out his chainmail. (How heavy it was! Lucky he only had a leather jerkin for protection.) Then he had to fetch out his horse's battle gear from its packing and polish the silver bosses and decorations, oil the leather and brush out the cloth and the tassels. Then groom the horse itself, a sweet grey beast called Sky who had no inkling he was going to war. Sigy was already moaning about leaving Aurelia behind, his darling. "What will she do without me?"

"Live in peace, you fool. Do you want her in the battle-lines? She's happy here."

As he brushed the little grey stallion Ed could not keep his excitement from welling up at the memory of Estrid's words. Alone now, he kept seeing again her bereft expression. For him! He was more thrilled with that than the thought of escaping. His life was turned upside down.

More than he knew.

It was October, the sweet sadness of autumn drifting over the marshes, with fire-smoke unmoving and the distant sea like a sheet of colourless metal. As the shadows grew long in the afternoon and the horses were all shining and fed, Ed straightened up from his tasks and saw Estrid coming from the store-shed, carrying a basket of vegetables. It was not her duty, and he knew at once that she was making an excuse. When she saw that he had seen her, she turned and went back into the shed. It was a plain invitation for him to follow.

Ed looked all round and saw no one particularly watching, only people going about their business and some girls playing with a rope. He wouldn't have another chance to speak to her. He turned and followed her into the shed.

She stood inside the door, waiting. When he approached her, they neither of them knew what to say. Her face flamed again, and he knew he was the same, the hot red in his cheeks as bright as his hair. He knew nothing about wooing, feeling only clumsy as an ox, yet longing to touch her. He did not dare. So they stood in the gloom of the store-shed, the playing girls' laughter pealing across the compound, the hammering of an anvil in the workshop echoing on the still air.

Gently she put out her hand and took the end of the belt that was hanging from his waist, and fingered the little golden heart. The belt was worn almost to a bare string, in spite of Ed's efforts to lengthen its life.

"You must come back, and bring me this," she said.

She spoke in her own language, which Ed now understood as well as his own.

He could not say anything, aware of his voice so rough, unable to spin fine words. She put out her hand, and he took it in his great dirty palm, ashamed. When he looked down her hand was like a white flower in his own dirty, crack-nailed mitt. He could not have said anything now even if he had wanted. He was trembling with the fires of love. And he a warrior tomorrow! The world was spinning round his head.

At that moment Sigy came to the door and hissed into the gloom, "Ohtar is coming!" Then he ran.

Estrid let out a cry of dismay and snatched back her hand. Ed stumbled back amongst the flour sacks, startled out of his dreaming. His anger and hatred flared as the doorway darkened and Ohtar's bulk blotted out the light.

"Estrid!"

He stepped in, snatched her arm, pulling her violently out of the gloom.

"I knew it!"

He swung round and saw Ed.

"You flame-haired cur!"

The foreign swear words poured over the boy's head, the rich invective laced with an evil satisfaction. His hand, like iron, closed over Ed's wrist, almost crunching the bones. Thank Christ the glorious sword was set out with his mail and helmet for the morning in the longhouse! Ed's thoughts flickered wildly, remembering Sigy's hand thrown to the dogs.

Ohtar's bellowing brought everyone out to see what was happening. He dragged the two of them ignominiously across the compound, then flung Estrid aside so that she almost fell. Hilde came running up to take her in her arms, then Ragnar and Rollo and the mother, alarmed, hurried out. Ohtar shouted at them, and Ed thought his voice sounded more triumphant than angry ... then orders to his servant, and the servant went running and in a moment returned with the sword. He held it out, the gorgeous hilt uncovered so that the jewels glinted in the pallid light. Asser, Sigy ... the shining blade ready to find more blood, to do the job it had been so finely crafted for... Ed did not think for a moment he would be spared. He was unprepared for death, the incident having happened so quickly. He felt the sky had fallen on him.

The whole encampment had been murmuring with excitement and speculation but when the servant held out the sword a great hush fell, broken only by a scream from Estrid. She tore herself out of Hilde's arms and flung herself at Ohtar, beating him wildly with her fists.

The hubbub rose up again, and out of it Ragnar's voice, calm.

"Give it to me."

Ohtar looked at his father furiously. Ragnar held out his hand. "Do as I tell you. Give it to me." His voice was icy.

"You want your daughter defiled by a slave?"

"I am the judge of what happens here. You are not the master, yet. Give me the sword."

The servant looked anxiously at Ohtar, the sword still in his hands. Ed felt the golden topaz eyes watching him, aching to eat him up as he trembled in Ohtar's grip. Then he saw Ohtar nod angrily to the servant. The sword was handed over.

Ragnar said, "Punish him if you must. But remember he marches with you tomorrow. And he'll not be a warrior without hands."

He put out his hand towards Estrid and took her from Hilde, not ungently.

"And you, child, will be punished. Ohtar is not in the wrong. Come away and leave them. It's not your business to watch punishments."

He took the sword with him, and left Ohtar still glowering with frustration. Ed knew the gods smiled on him. He straightened up proudly. He was not optimistic about his future prospects but rejoiced to see the anger boiling in Ohtar's face. Not this time! he wanted to shout at him. He could not stop himself smiling, biting back jeering words. Do what you will! His defiance did his cause no good.

Ohtar ordered a tripod to be set up, the three legs wedged firmly in the ground in the middle of the compound. Then Ed's wrists were bound tightly behind his back and the rope thrown over the top of the tripod. With three slaves pulling, he was hoisted up into the air so that all his weight hung from his arms, twisted unnaturally in their shoulder sockets. It was extremely unpleasant.

As he hung there, revolving slowly in the evening breeze, Ohtar stood below him and laughed. The frustration and anger were wiped out, an almost kindly, expectant expression lighting his deepset eyes.

"It's not too bad for a few minutes. But after an hour – and then another – you will be sorry, Firehead, I promise you. In the morning you will be sorry."

He turned on his heel and strode away. Ed had no reason not to believe him. But there was very little he could do about it.

The sun slipped peacefully behind the trees and the air sharpened. The stars came out, and a fine sliver of a moon cast a surprising light. A guard of two men was set on Ed. They sat on the ground, playing a dice game, laughing occasionally. Sigy came out and sat with them, but not speaking with them, his back turned. Ed muttered at him to go back in, but he did not move. Eventually Ed could not speak, nor breathe, and wished his anguished hands had indeed been cut off, for it would have been merciful compared to this. He lost consciousness, and did not see Ohtar come out to enjoy looking on his blue-white face in the moonlight, the fiery hair lank and dishevelled with pain, the strangled hands bloodless under the cords.

"Cut him down," he said to the men.

Sigy leapt up to catch Ed's body as the men sawed the cords, but Ohtar kicked him away and the body fell in a heap.

"Get to bed, all of you. The dogs will watch him." He hit Sigy and Sigy ran. Ohtar's two dogs, evil and vicious like their master, were ordered, "Watch!" and sat waiting for signs of life from the still body while Ohtar went in to sleep.

Chapter 8

Sigy was good with animals. He wooed the dogs with bits of dried meat he got from the store and spoke to them for a long time in a gentle voice. When at last he felt it safe to touch Ed the dogs watched him but merely growled. Sigy recognized these as token growls. Ed's eyes were open but he could not move. Sigy fetched his sheepskin from the snoring slave bench and put it over him and sat with him under the shadow of the tripod, listening to the night cries of the waders out on the marshes and stroking the dogs. It was cold and sharp. Sigy thought, we might soon be dead. What does it matter?

Some time before dawn he was able to help Ed to his feet. Ed's arms hurt him so much that Sigy could not get them over his shoulders to support him, but had to some-how hold him round the waist and guide his staggering steps into the longhouse. There he lay until dawn, in great pain, while Sigy lay close trying to warm him. When the slaves got up to start feeding the animals Sigy stayed, and Thored brought him some gruel with warm milk to feed to Ed.

The day was fine and the settlement humming with excitement at the warriors' departure. The horses were whinnying, dogs barking. Rollo wanted his horse prepared and Sigy had to run. Ed struggled to follow him, but it was all he could do to sit up, let alone stand. The view down the longhouse kept coming and going and a terrible noise buzzed in his ears. Out of his crazed vision he saw Ohtar approaching, dressed in all his warrior's finery with a bronze helmet on his head. At his side was the beautiful sword, and in his hand a sharp dagger.

He stood looking down on Ed, smiling.

"My sister thinks you are very handsome. I think we will change that, so that her eyes will not want to linger on you any longer."

Ed scarcely comprehended what he said. But as Ohtar raised the dagger he thought he was going to cut his nose off, the commonest and most disgusting of all the mutilations practised on wrongdoers. He cowered back. Ohtar caught him viciously by the hair and forced his head back, and with the point of the dagger made two deep incisions down Ed's cheeks. Ed had a close-up view of the blond hairs in Ohtar's nostrils and the thick pulsing tendons in his neck as he laughed, and felt the hot blood pouring down his face.

"And your beautiful hair!"

Ohtar laughed again. Jerking up handfuls of hair from Ed's head, he sawed it all off close to the scalp.

Ed's vision dissolved in bright tears of rage and agony. A sea of darkness washed over him. He felt himself fighting to keep above the waves, but hands held him down. The fresh pain in his face battled with the awful throbbing of his shoulders and chest. And he had been going to fight ... the greatest day of his life ... and Estrid ... Estrid...!

He heard Rollo shouting and Ohtar still laughing, and a lot of commotion. Sigurd was doing something to his face... He tried to wrest himself away, it hurt so much, but hands held him down.

"Sigy! Sigy!"

But Ohtar knocked Sigy away, and bellowed at them all to go. They were leaving. Had they all forgotten there was a battle to fight?

"And you too, my fine lad – you'll not be

left behind to make sheep's eyes at my sister! Hurry up, Sigurd, the boy will hold us up."

"The boy can't walk," Sigurd said.

"He can ride," Ohtar said curtly, "until he's fit. If Rollo wants him, Rollo can take him."

And so Ed lurched out of the settlement riding behind Rollo on the little horse he had so diligently groomed the day before, barely conscious. Rollo was worried about blood on his new surcoat and the women gave Ed cloths for his face. Some of them were crying, and Ed heard one say, "God bless Cnut, for taking Ohtar away!" and another, "He'll get no worse wounds in battle, and all for a calf love!"

It was all Ed could do to stop from dropping off the horse's back, but the pace was gentle and gradually, as the sun warmed his aching back, he started to come to and gather his wits together. He wanted to feel his face but he could not lift his hands up. What had Ohtar done to him? But at least, not his nose ... noseless people looked vile, and were seen often enough, earless as well. Whatever Ohtar had done, it wasn't as bad as cutting off his nose. And his hair – well, that was nothing, save for seeing Ohtar laughing as he wielded the dagger. And his hate for Ohtar rose up in

Ed's throat like a sick bile, choking him. One day he would kill Ohtar with his own hands, whether in battle or in peace. Everybody hated him, even his own father. And he, Edmund, hated him beyond endurance. Whatever was to happen, he would get his revenge, sooner or later.

The day, for Ed, passed in a haze, and when they stopped to make camp at night he fell asleep on the ground where he dropped. The pace had been easy, to accommodate the walking slaves. They were all promised their freedom and land if they fought well. Most of them were willing to turn Dane for this opportunity but Sigy, lying beside Ed, could not see how he could do it. Fight for Ohtar! Fight against his own kind, perhaps against these brothers of Ed's that he spoke of so often – it wasn't possible!

But even if Ed was capable, there was no way of escaping with Ohtar's dogs on watch. The two dogs Sigy had made friends with had been joined by four more, and even to get up to relieve oneself was fraught with danger. Sigy lay looking at the stars, wondering what was to become of them. He knew nothing about fighting.

Cnut had lost the last battle, and was

thought to be making for his ships which lay on the Thames. Edmund Ironsides was said to be in pursuit. News was hard to come by, and Ohtar had sent two scouts on ahead to the nearest fort to see if he could get word. They would stay where they were until the scouts returned.

Sigy was too worried to sleep. He was used to Ed making the decisions but Ed wasn't going to make any decisions for some time. What a mess Ohtar had made of him! The wounds in his cheeks were deep and would leave terrible scars, even though dragged together with Sigurd's rough stitchery, and the hacked hair looked like a drunken peasant's hayfield. But for Ed, Sigy knew he would have lost both hands and been turned out as a beggar or to die. Sigy would die now for Ed, but not for a crowd of stupid fighting Danes.

"What shall we do?" he whispered to Ed when Ed was capable of making sense.

"Did you get the spearheads?"

"Yes. They're under my tunic, strapped to my thigh."

"We'll have to seize a chance if it turns up. It might not. I'm not fighting for the Danes, whatever the others choose."

"We'll have to line up and show willing.

81

Then in the confusion of the fighting we can slide off and hide."

"Not get parted, whatever happens."

"Never!"

"What do I look like, Sigy?"

"A piece of tapestry." Sigy laughed. "Estrid loves tapestry."

"Oh, Estrid!" Ed groaned. "She came to me, Sigy. It wasn't me – I didn't – " He groaned again. What was the use? He didn't expect to return to Ragnar's settlement. He had dreamed of his own family, his mother and Oswy. Perhaps Oswy was fighting now, as well as Wistan and Godric. That was the side he should be on!

He knew that Ohtar, having offered freedom and land to the slaves if they fought, would not include him in the deal. Sigy perhaps, but not him.

They heard one of Ohtar's bodyguard say, "The armies are equally matched. This fighting gets us nowhere. They should make a treaty."

"Cnut is making for his ships. If we're defeated again, we'll be heading for home."

"If we're lucky enough!"

Ed and Sigy thought that if luck went against them they might end up rowing the Danes back across the sea. But Ed smiled –

how it hurt! – and said, "Not you, Sigy. You'd be useless rowing."

"I'll go back to my granny," Sigy said.

It was comforting to think of grannies and mothers and their old place in their own families, lying in the night on the brink of going to battle. Yet there was a deep vein of excitement underneath the nostalgia. Nobody slept soundly, feeling close to momentous happenings. And in the morning when the scouts reported back they were roused back on to the road and the pace was now urgent. The slaves had to jogtrot. Ed rode behind Rollo again.

They came to a river but it was too full to cross and they had to wait for the tide to ebb. Ohtar sat impatiently on his horse at the ford, scowling. The few huts and hovels on the other side of the river were deserted, or perhaps the peasants were hiding up. These were the people Ohtar would rob for food and forage for the horses when he was on the march – no wonder the poor devils kept their heads down. Sigy remembered this was how he had been caught, by just such a scavenging party. Now he was one of them.

But as they waited there came a sort of murmur on the air. The gulls flew up, squawking. One of their horses whinnied. Ed felt his insides stiffen with excitement. He could hear the throb of hooves and distant jingle of bit and chain, and on the far bank, up river, a banner fluttered above the thorn-scrub...

"Let's hope it's Cnut and not Ironsides," one of the slaves muttered.

An army on the march... Even with his mixed feelings Ed could not help but be stirred by the sight of the outriders as they came along the opposite bank, followed first by the horsemen and then by the foot soldiers, miles of them, it seemed, tailing away into the far distance. The riders wore helmets and mail and tunics, once white, and carried shields and spears, and their horses were decked out like Rollo's Sky in silver-chased bridles and fluttering saddle-cloths. But the foot soldiers were less grand and infinitely weary, stumbling along in the mud carved up by the horses ahead. War-scarred and bitter, only their numbers were impressive. This was one of the most successful armies to attack Britain, but it had been beaten in its last battle and after a year of fighting was at the end of its tether.

Leading them, surrounded by his bodyguard, was the famed Cnut, son of the notorious Sven Forkbeard. He was only in his young twenties but had forged a legend of invincibility, scourging the country from Lundenburg to York, from Gloucester to Essex. Nothing had stopped him until Edmund Ironsides had taken over from his weak father and started to carve out a similar reputation.

When the outriders came to the ford they hailed Ohtar and Ohtar shouted back his name, proudly.

"Come to serve our King!"

One of the horsemen came forward and shouted, "You're not much good on that side of the river! Can you cross?"

Several horsemen came to help, for the water was still deep and the current ran rapidly. Sigy hung on to Rollo's stirrup and was still almost swept off his feet, and one slave in spite of the horsemen lost his footing and was swept downstream, bobbing and screaming. Nobody bothered to save him – it was too much trouble. Ohtar, with only his feet wet, was greeted warmly, and Rollo went up behind him to be acknowledged by the famous warrior.

Ed, looking over Rollo's shoulder, saw the sky-blue eyes of the Danish warlord resting on him curiously. Cnut was tall and fair and extremely handsome, a natural hero, and Ed at that moment wished he felt he could give him allegiance. Especially when he said to Rollo, "You are kind to your servant. Does he always ride behind?"

Rollo went scarlet and stammered, "N-no, my lord. But he is injured."

"So I see."

And Ed wished he could see what he saw – a piece of tapestry? – and coloured up as badly as Rollo.

"Not by chance, I think."

Ohtar growled, "He deserved worse, my lord. But he will make another soldier tomorrow."

"We might need him tomorrow," Cnut said. "The English king is on our heels and coming fast. We are going to have to stand and fight. I am glad to see you again, Ohtar. You've timed it well."

And the army moved off again, Ohtar and Rollo riding behind Cnut amongst the other horsemen and the slaves falling in behind. Ed was anxious not to be parted from Sigy, but relied on Sigy to keep track of Sky, whose grey colouring stood out from most of the other horses. This would be his last ride, he knew, for his strength was returning. His arms were starting to work again, although not without crucifying pain.

They marched until late afternoon, following the south bank of the river, then stopped to camp. Scouts reported Ironsides still twenty miles away and Cnut decided that no battle would be joined until morning. His army badly needed rest. Such was their discipline, they had wood cut and fires burning in no time, and the packhorses at the end of the line were unloaded of the various sheep, bullocks and pigs that had been slaughtered along the way to feed them. The horses were turned loose to graze.

Ohtar and Rollo were to eat with Cnut's party. Rollo steadied Ed as he slid painfully to the ground.

"Sometimes I hate Ohtar as much as you do," he said quietly.

"You have no cause. I have cause."

"I could order you not to fight tomorrow."

"No! That would be no favour!" Ed was startled. In the mêlée of battle he and Sigy would engineer their escape – although how it might come about was impossible to foresee.

Rollo was not stupid. He suspected Ed's intentions.

"You will not fight your own kind? Not even for your freedom?"

"Ohtar will never give me my freedom, not if I kill Ironsides himself."

Rollo sighed. "No, I think not." Then he smiled. "But I would, if Ohtar is killed."

Ed said, "If I kill him?" He tried to smile, but it hurt too much.

"No. Not if you kill him. Then I would have you killed too. But if, in fair battle, Ohtar is killed, then I give the orders. I would give you whatever you want, Edmund, although I would rather keep you by my side."

"I would serve you as a free man. Not as a slave. Unless – " He shrugged (which was another painful mistake). "We don't know – "

"We might both be dead tomorrow."

"Yes."

They both grinned then, a hollow gesture. And Rollo's grin faded and he suddenly looked what he truly felt – very frightened.

"I suppose, in the heat of battle, I might prove brave enough – I've heard them talk often enough of how the spirit leaps, the gods give strength, when the enemy is at hand. I would not miss it. But – " He shook his head. "It's the ship I care about, my father's ship. I would sail the ship for Cnut to the ends of the earth, happily – that is what I want most."

It was Rollo who had kept the ship sound and cossetted over its years on the shore. Ohtar had never looked at it, and Ragnar rarely. To them it had served its purpose, conveying them to Britain.

"If I come out of this tomorrow I shall ask my father if I can offer Cnut our ship, with me as its sailing-master. That's what I really want."

Cnut had over forty ships of war lying off the south coast.

Ed remembered his first sight of Rollo four years ago – his startled glimpse of the blond boy standing at the steering-board of the great ship as it ploughed before the wind in the swirling mist – how proud and exultant his stance, making land at last. But the sea had no attraction for Ed. He had seen it in all its moods ever since he was born, but never felt its attraction.

"I pray you get your wish."

It was the parting of the ways now, quite likely for ever. Ed hesitated, but slaves had no call to embrace or show emotion. He liked Rollo. He could not show it.

"Your God keep you, Edmund."

"And you."

He went to find Sigy, shaken by the parting. Sigy was grumbling.

"A decent man would see to his slaves before sitting down himself," he said. "Ohtar has abandoned us. He treats his horses better."

But a kindly, elderly soldier gave them space at his fire, and when the meat was cut they got a share. They ate ravenously and lay down with the others by the fire, pulling their cloaks close as the autumn night sharpened the air. There were no plans to be made, for who knew what was going to happen?

Chapter 9

"I don't know why we bother about who we are loyal to. Half these men are Russians or Celts, or from Mercia or Wessex. You're hard put to it to find a Dane."

Sigy made this discovery when he woke up and went to forage for bread and ale. Ed was so stiff he could scarcely move. His cheeks stung in the cold wind. He pulled his leather cap down closely. It was scarcely dawn and the skylarks were singing as if it were midsummer. Some soldiers still snored soundly and he wished he could be as unconcerned.

He had already discovered that several of his companions were as native as he was.

"We'll fight for anyone as'll feed us," an elderly man laughed. But his grandfather had come over to settle and he came from a close Danish community in Mercia. He could not speak the language as well as either Ed or Sigy, but his allegiance was to Cnut.

"He's a fine man, just and strong. Cnut'll make a good king."

Other opinions were offered.

"Edmund Ironsides is a fine man too."

"Aye, well, they should divide. We're equally matched."

"Today might settle it."

"At least I stay on the same side. There's some as'll jump sides, whoever's winning. Ironsides has Eadric on his side today, who twice has fought with us. He's an evil, slippery cur if ever there was one."

When they were scoffing their bread together, Ed said, "It's nothing like I thought. If we change sides, no one will notice. I'm no Dane. I can't kill anyone of my own kin."

"I don't think I can kill anyone at all," Sigy said.

"We've not been trained. But I'm sure it's not difficult." Ed was thinking of Ohtar, and having the Roman spear in his hand. (If his hand had the power to throw, which he doubted.)

There were no weapons for them – "Take them from the other side!" they were instructed – so Sigy scrounged two spear-shafts and they fixed their Roman spearheads to them with twine. The elderly soldier scoffed at what he saw as their eagerness and said, "That's fine, but where are your shields?"

There were not enough to go round.

"When the arrows come over, you duck down hard behind the man in front of you," the soldier advised. "Otherwise the day will be over before it's started."

As they looked so blank, he said, "Each side sends a shower of arrows first. It thins the ranks out nicely. And then it's in and chop, man to man."

He had a two-edged axe.

Sigy looked palely at Ed. They both realized how sheltered their life had been under the kindly Ragnar.

It was a cool grey morning. The scouts had ridden in with news that Edmund's army had camped seven miles back and was now on the march. A commander came through the camp rousting everyone up, the fires were put out and the men got themselves into fighting order. Cloaks were discarded, leather jerkins and helmets pulled tight. The horses were chased away out of danger, for they took no part in the fighting – Cnut and Ironsides himself fought hand to hand like their men. Ed saw Ohtar with his sword unsheathed, and Rollo at his side as pale as death. Cnut, like many of the Danes, was a tall man and stood out amongst his bodyguard, his fair head covered with a gorgeous bronze helmet. He was no leader from behind, but a man with a reputation for bravery and inspiring valour. Seeing him, Ed wished he could give him his loyalty. But loyalty was to one's kind.

An old priest doddered out and quavered some prayers over them so that the Christians amongst them could feel blessed. Cnut bowed his head gravely. Unlike his father, he was ready to tailor his religion to his best interests. He wanted to be king of England and to be a Christian was necessary.

Whoever was God, Ed and Sigy prayed to him fervently.

The man beside Ed crossed himself and said, "We need prayers. We've been defeated the last three times we met."

Edmund and Sigy exchanged glances. No one had told them this. Ohtar was so full of bravado they had assumed that his side was the winning one. Was this the last stand, before Cnut took ignominious retreat to his ships and sailed away? Looking at him, Ed found this hard to believe.

Now, as they lined up in battle formation, they noticed that all the men had gone quiet. Their faces were taut and grim. Ed and Sigy found themselves near the back of the vast wedge of men; the place at the point in front was taken by Cnut himself, surrounded by a bodyguard of the tallest warriors. They wriggled themselves in behind two large men who carried round shields. Not every soldier had a shield, although all had an axe or a spear. Some had both. Ed wasn't sure how well he had bound his spearhead to the haft, and shivered at the thought of plunging it into a man. It might be Wistan or Godric ahead of him, his own mother's sons. . .

The man next to him said, "It's every man for himself when the fighting starts, trying not to get killed. Keep your heads down, lads, don't go looking for glory. There's another day, remember."

What sort of encouragement was that?

"If we get parted," Sigy said, "we must make a place – "

"To meet. Afterwards. That hilltop, say – "

They were marching now, and the hilltop was ahead of them, cutting off the view to the west. The ground was goat-grazed and rough, but there were no trees here – they had been taken for fuel. Once on the ridge ahead, surely they would see Ironsides' army coming to meet them?

Ed's breath came quickly, half weakness,

half excitement, and the thick smell of sweat and dirt and damp leather filled his nostrils as the pace increased. There was a palpable rising of tension in the close-packed ranks, muttered praying and a good deal of profanity. Crude jokes were bandied as a way of keeping up spirits. Fear surged but was spiked through with a strange and wild excitement that drove the body forward. Ed had never known such a weird feeling as infected him now, having no choice in his actions yet not wanting, suddenly, for it to be any different. Life had never been on this plane before. He glanced at Sigy and saw the light in his eyes and bright colour in his cheeks. He was enjoying himself!

A ragged shout went up from the head of the column and the pace suddenly slackened. Looking up over the burly shoulders in front of him, Ed saw figures breasting the hilltop they were facing. The sun glanced off steel in a flurry of twinkling light, a bright standard rippled against the sky and suddenly the hilltop seemed to come alive like an ant-heap. Hundreds of men were coming over the top.

"Oh, help us, Christ!" the man next to Ed prayed, and crossed himself. He started to run. Ed had to run too, pressed from behind. He saw Cnut's standard break out ahead of him, a lot of the men were shouting. With

Ironsides' men coming towards them the valley between seemed to shrink rapidly. A shout came from ahead, and they all crashed to a halt. The bowmen took up their stance and there was a sudden tense silence. Ed couldn't see what was happening, crouched close behind the large frame of the smelly soldier in front of him who was swinging his shield to the front. He heard a skylark singing, and some gulls quarrelling across the river as if this day was no different from any other. For them, perhaps, it wasn't.

But Ed had never heard such a sound as now filled the sky, like a great sigh winging up from the hillside. The sound of a thousand arrows was like the passage of a thousand birds, flying faster than ever a bird could fly and with a beak more terrible than any bird could boast. The arrowheads were made by craftsmen whose skill was legendary – Ed remembered in that moment Wistan once showing him how they were fashioned. The thud of their deadly points drummed against the roof of shields but the noise was immediately drowned by terrible screams and shouting.

And then they were running again, and stumbling over fallen bodies, and screams and groans seemed to come from underfoot. And beside Ed the praying soldier was now blaspheming and had his terrible axe in both hands, and he was no longer advising Ed but intent only on landing the first blow.

And now, as he jumped over writhing bodies, Ed saw the first enemy in front of him, a chest instead of a back, and a face twisted with hate and pure fear, the eyes bulging, lips wrenched back. Ed lifted his spear, feeling like a sparrow before an enormous cat, but the man went straight past him and lunged at the Dane behind him who sidestepped and swung his axe. Ed heard a crack like a loud whiplash and the man's leg soared up in the air, unattached, making a fine arc, and rolled across the ground in front of Ed. Ed jumped over it. He felt as if his hair was literally standing on end, the horror of what he saw all round him blinding him to any sense of reality. A man had an axehead buried in his scalp, cleaving a chasm between his two eyes, and was standing swaying with a smile like a rivet still joining the bottom half of his face. And another man beside him had no head at all, but seemed to take all the time in the world to fall, his great hands hanging loose and his shield and spear falling from his grasp to hit the ground before him.

Ed dodged, ran. Where? Up the hill, it

seemed safer. But someone crossed his path, a slender boy with a slender spear which Ed knocked out of his hand with his own. The boy screamed. He was more frightened than Ed himself. Ed was going to spin round and spear him properly, uplifted by his own sudden supremacy, but then he remembered that he intended to fight on the same side as this boy, the side of his people. But now it came to the point, in the mêlée it was hard to see quickly enough who was friend and who was foe before the blade fell. Ed found his spear hard to wield with his hopelessly weak arms and when he saw a sword lying on the ground he flung the spear aside and grabbed it. It was heavy and felt more useful but the strained muscles of his arms trembled at the weight.

No sooner had he picked it up than someone came at him with a spear. The arms which felt so hopeless were galvanized into sudden health and raised the blade in time to deflect the deadly shaft. Knocked off course, it fell to lodge in the leg of a man behind him who dropped to the ground with a roar of pain and anger. Ed ran. What was he doing here? He had no idea how to use this sword he clutched so convulsively in both hands.

A cluster of old hawthorn bushes stood in his path and he ducked beneath the spiny branches and stood for a moment with his back to the trunks, trying to gain his breath and his wits. The whole side of the hill was a mass of heaving, hacking bodies and the air was rent with terrible cries and screaming, but the sun was shining and below in the valley the fields were bathed in a soft autumn light and some cows were grazing peacefully by the waterside. There was even a little fishing boat out on the water, and some gulls trailing it. Ed saw this scene as if it was quite separate from the world he was part of. And so it was – so close, and yet like paradise and just as unattainable. And even as he crouched there beneath the tree, a man like an ox came at him with sword drawn, and grabbed him with an enormous hand. He pulled him out like a rabbit from a hole and held him tight by the front of his leather jerkin. He raised his sword and Ed wriggled furiously. "Don't kill me – I'm a Saxon!"

"This is a Dane's jerkin!"

"Do I sound like a Dane?"

The man threw him to one side with such force that Ed might as well have been pole-axed, his head slammed against the tree trunk. He lay with swimming brains, unable to move. When his senses returned he wondered whether it was worth it, to brave again the carnage that was none of his business. The English seemed to be moving down the hill and forcing the Danes back, and if he lay where he was the battle would move past him. Then he would be in the right place and on the winning side. No one was taking any notice of him at all, hidden as he was amongst the bushes.

Nearest to him the fighting was fairly even and some of his own companions were holding off the men coming down the hill. The leader of Ironsides' men on this side was a thickset, dark-haired man in a surcoat and helmet that showed high rank. His men fought well, but their leader suddenly turned away from the fray and started running back up the hill. Ed thought it must be some sort of ploy, a trick, but in a moment all his men, seeing the retreat, turned and followed him, and it no longer looked like a trick, but a plain act of funk.

It left a large swathe of Ironsides' right flank entirely unprotected, and Cnut's men came bounding up the hill with triumphant cries to fill the gap. Amongst the mêlée Ed suddenly caught sight of Sigy.

He leapt to his feet and ran out, shouting after him. Sigy glanced round and yelled back, and then they were together again and running, surrounded by blood-lusting Danes swinging their axes. Ed knew he was mad, but at that moment he was happy. All his doubts about whose side he was on seemed to evaporate into the quivering air – he was on the winning side, and would kill whoever crossed him! Kill or be killed – that was the only way to think. Skiving under the bushes would gain him nothing.

Sigy was actually laughing.

Ed saw him lift his spear and ram it into a man half-turned, already fighting with somebody else. It went right through the man's shoulder and out the other side. He went down like a falling stone, while the man he was fighting stumbled over the body and fell flat on his face. Sigy had a job pulling the spear free and was for a moment unguarded. Seeing it, a white-faced youth came at him with a sword, but Ed leapt forward and with his own sword knocked the weapon right out of the boy's hand. The boy screamed. Ed flailed at him wildly, his blood racing with a mad excitement. But he had no expertise and his arms no strength after their treatment from Ohtar. When the boy ducked Ed's lunge met no resistance. He was carried by his own impetus and fell in a heap. A very large man then came down behind the boy and shouted, "Leave him to me!"

Ed saw the sudden flash of light on the sword as it was raised above him. He rolled over and grabbed at the man's ankle, but the man stamped on his wrist and held him pinned. He was laughing. The sword caught the sun again.

"*No!*"

Was it him or Sigy screaming? Or both?

Sigy had freed his spear but had no time to take more than a wild aim. The point hit the man in the thigh and brought him down. He roared like a stuck pig but even from the ground swung with his sword. Suddenly freed, Ed leapt up and nimbly dodged the wild swipe. Sigy jabbed again, freed his spear and shouted, "Run!"

They ran. Leaping and shrieking up the hill, over bodies and sliding in blood-soaked grass. But men stood before them, not running. Sigy dodged, but Ed caught the full force of an ash stave in his chest and spun round, all his breath punctured. The sky spun. His living breath deserted him, yet he could still see. Connect. Think. Another man with a sword – was there no end to them? – he rolled away and saw the flash of sun on steel yet again. He groaned, kicked out like a felled ox, staggered to his feet. The man with the sword had gone – where? – why? – Ed had no idea. Sigy screamed at him, "Come on!"

And then it all happened again, so fast it was hard to take in. The flash of sun on a sword. Ed felt something hit him in the back of the neck, saw Sigy's spear fly up in the air. Sigy went down and the sword fire flashed over his head. Ed lunged, two-handed. His sword entered flesh, a roar of pain almost deafened him. But the sword wavered. Fell.

Sigy screamed.

But this time in agony. Ed's blood ran cold in that second.

Sigy fell and Ed caught him, spinning sideways to the ground with Sigy in his arms. Feet kicked them and stumbled over them as they rolled across the turf.

Ed shut his eyes, not wanting to see, listening to the echoes of the cries across the top of the hill. He did not dare look at Sigy. He was trembling with the horror of what had happened.

Sigy moaned, tried to sit up, and found he had no arm to propel him. He had no arms at all.

He looked surprised, bewildered, then blank. Ed turned and saw the brightness fade from his face. His eyes stared, black pits of horror.

"Ed!"

But Ed could find nothing to say. His horror was as great as Sigy's. He wrapped his arms round Sigy and cradled him, and Sigy started to moan, "Kill me, Ed. Kill me."

Ed longed for someone to help, for Sigurd, for Thored, anybody, but the fighting had now passed on and was disappearing over the hill. The wide river valley was now empty save for the swathes of bodies lying across its slopes. The man who, Ed presumed, had attacked Sigy was lying with Ed's sword sticking out of his belly. He was still alive, but beyond caring.

Ed, after a little while, thought perhaps he should try and staunch the blood from Sigy's wound, but Sigy, while he had the strength, wouldn't let him.

"Don't touch me!"

He was white to the lips. Perhaps it was best that he should die like this. It was a kind enough death, to bleed away.

But triumphant soldiers were coming back to pick over the dead and claim their prizes. There was a lot of shouting and jubilation, and quarrelling, as bodies were stripped of gold rings and jewellery and good shoes and valuable chainmail. Ed noticed that most of the badly wounded were dispatched where they lay with a thrust of sword or spear. He hadn't the stomach to retrieve his sword from the man's belly, but groped for Sigy's dropped spear as a protection. He knew, if he had any sense, he should get up and run, but the booty-hunting men were Danes and he could speak to them in their own language. He had fought with them, after all, as much as he had fought at all.

A party of Ironsides' men was coming back to retrieve their dead. The fighting seemed to be finished, for they were not apprehended by the foraging Danes.

Whatever might happen, Ed would not leave Sigy. Sigy lay with his head on Ed's chest, his eyes shut, although he was not unconscious. His breathing was light and slow. Ed felt the tears running down his cheeks, more for his own loss than Sigy's plight. A looting party was coming nearer. Ed heard a familiar hoarse laugh, and his heart lurched unpleasantly. It was Ohtar, with four of his henchmen. Ed had hoped fervently that Ohtar had been killed, but luck had favoured the undeserving. Ed did not move.

Ohtar saw him, just when Ed thought he had been overlooked. About to carry on down the hill, Ohtar looked back and saw the bright remains of Ed's hacked hair on what he thought were dead bodies. He turned back to investigate. Ed saw the pleasure break across his face as he came near and recognized the two of them.

"So, my sister's darling!"

He had his sword in his hand, and the blade was red with blood. He pointed it at Sigy and said, "He's no use now, even to himself," and thrust it deeply into Sigy's chest. Sigy died instantly.

Ed held the body close, shaking.

The sword point flicked his shoulders, carving gouts of blood.

"Get up."

Ed knew that Ohtar was going to kill him. With the light gone out of Sigy, he did not care. He laid Sigy gently away from him and stumbled to his feet.

"I don't want you crying home to my sister," Ohtar sneered. "Another body here will go unremarked, I think."

Ed never forgot the look of pleasure and excitement in Ohtar's eyes. Ohtar's eyes were a dark blue, and his brows and hair were much darker than Rollo's. His chin was heavy and tending to jowls.

Ed stood square before him and thought, "I'm coming too, Sigy. We'll be together," and felt no fear.

But a voice broke in, so familiar that Ed jumped.

"The killing is over. Put up your sword, or you'll have mine across your throat."

A tall, bare-headed man stood behind Ed, facing Ohtar. He had a sword in his hand that was bloodier than Ohtar's.

It was Wistan.

Chapter 10

As Ed let out a strangled cry of recognition Wistan turned from Ohtar, astonished. His stern face cleared momentarily.

"Firehead?"

"Wistan!"

Crazed from Sigy's death, Ed flung himself into Wistan's embrace without a thought for rank or situation, nearly knocking him off his feet. Wistan's appearance at that moment was as if God himself had come down from Heaven. Wistan held him tightly, but his sword still pointed at Ohtar, who was gaping at the turn of events.

Wistan said, "This is my brother. Take another step and I shall kill you."

Ohtar said, "Your brother is my slave. He is my property, to do as I like with."

Ohtar had four men with him and Wiston was alone, but he did not flinch.

"I am here under your king's command to mark the Saxon dead. You will answer to Cnut if you cross me. Get on your way. Your slave will stay with me."

Ohtar dropped his sword's point and stood looking doubtful. Then his henchmen came forward and muttered to him, obviously wishing to withdraw, and Ohtar swore and turned away. The five of them went marching away across the hillside.

"So." Wistan held Ed away from him, looking closely at his sewn-together face. "Who did this to you? Even slaves don't deserve such treatment."

"He did. And he killed Sigy." The tears poured down Ed's cheeks as he turned from Wistan to the body of his friend. Sigy seemed to be smiling, lying lazily as if he were asleep. His eyes were open but no light shone in them. His careless brown curls lifted in the afternoon breeze.

Wistan put his arm round Ed's shoulders. "Perhaps it is the best way. A man without arms has no life, after all."

"He said, kill me. But I would have looked after him, always. I would have been his arms," Ed sobbed.

"Come, Ed. He is in good company. Half our great men have been slain on this hillside today. I think today marks the end for us. We might all be slaves before we're through."

"I can't leave him."

"My men will bury him for you, Edmund, I promise. I'll send a party down and you can direct them. But we have to carry our elder-men away. Ulfcytel is killed, and Aelfric and Aethelweard, so many great men . . . you must help me."

It dawned on Ed gradually as the afternoon unfolded that his brother Wistan was a trusted courtier of the defeated King Edmund as well as a soldier. He had been commanded to collect the bodies of all the high-ranking warriors before the corpse robbers defiled them and the circling crows pecked out their eyes. Men came down the hill with hurdles to carry away the bodies as Wistan walked amongst the piles of corpses, marking the ones destined for more than a common grave.

Ed kept by his side. Although he had recognized his brother readily enough, the Wistan Ed remembered was a far cry from this stern warrior. Wistan was now a man, battle-hardened. The laughing face was lined already, the smiles had vanished, the eyes grown cautious and full of pain. Only his quick, lithe movements were the same, and his scornful air of authority.

"This is a bad day for us, my Firehead. Save for meeting up with you." And he smiled his rare smile. "What news have you of our parents?"

Ed told him what had happened. Wistan said that Godric had been killed in battle in Lincolnshire two years ago.

"And this armless friend of yours?"

Ed explained that too. "He is my other part, and I his. Since we were taken."

In the evening two men with spades followed Ed down to where Sigy lay, and at least he got a grave, which was more than most managed. Ed laid his lovely Roman spearhead beside him, about the only possession he had ever boasted – for who knew what one might need in the life beyond? – and put a bunch of wild roses on his breast. And when the grave was covered he borrowed a spade to dig up the wild rose bush and plant it at Sigy's head, so that one day he might come back and find Sigy flowering in the sunshine. He would always remember Sigy laughing. Even being a one-handed slave had rarely doused his spirits.

The shock and grief of losing Sigy countered the joy of finding Wistan. Without Wistan he felt he might well have crawled back to Ohtar like a dog to be fed and housed and beaten. But with Wistan protecting him a whole new scene opened up before him. If only Sigy were there to share it!

That night he lay down with Wistan and his men on the top of the hill. His whole body ached appallingly but the excitements of the day buzzed in his head so that he could not sleep. The horrors he had seen tormented him. The moon came out and shone serenely over the wide valley, silvering the path of the meandering river and blanching the faces of the dead. The badly wounded had all been dispatched like Sigy, others carted and dragged away by their friends, probably to die more slowly on the cold hillside. The light of several small fires flickered where men huddled and the smell of blood and trampled mud mingled with the sweet smell of wood-smoke.

He slept, eventually, and was woken at dawn by Wistan. The plans were to march for Lundenburg and then westward to follow King Edmund and the remains of his army.

"He is heading for home, fast, to make Cnut follow him. He will have to treaty with Cnut and he wants the treatying to take place on his own ground, in the west. There is no more army left to fight with," Wistan said heavily.

"Your army was coming down the hill," Ed said. "And then the leader on the left flank turned and fled and all his men followed him. And Cnut's men broke through and pushed your army back."

"So I believe."

Wistan's face glowered. He was still a young man but the responsibilities he bore had given him the stature of someone much older. Ed was nervous of him, seeing the authority he had over his companions. He was like Oswy in appearance, but far better looking, still the hero figure that Ed remembered, with his dark, tousled hair and sharp, dark blue eyes. He had always been impatient of peasant life, Ed remembered, and had wandered widely before departing for good. Their father had never had any say over him.

"We know who is responsible, never fear. The King was mad to take him back, after he had betrayed us twice already – friend Eadric. He likes power, but is a mortal coward when it comes to fighting. Then with sweet words he gets back in favour. He is as slippery as an eel. A viper, rather. He lost us the day. The kingdom."

Wistan gazed away down the valley, full of mist and the first birdsong. Ed found it hard to remember what had happened, where he was. But Wistan was his saviour.

"Are you coming with me?" Wistan asked him.

"Yes!"

"It will be hard. You know that? We are in no position now to make the rules. That master of yours with the fine sword is on the winning side, and might yet be telling us what to do. You might be better a slave with him than a free man with your brother."

"No! He's another viper! His father's not, and his brother's all right, but Ohtar is a vile man. A viper like Eadric."

Wistan laughed. "They are friends, I believe. When Eadric decided to be on their side, Ohtar was his friend. I recognized Ohtar yesterday, when he had his sword-point at your chest."

They made ready to depart, which took no time as they had no possessions. The Danes had taken their horses. With Ed there were seven in the party. Wistan was in charge, with a swarthy young man called Aelfric – or Fric – as his second-in-command.

They crossed over the top of the hill and marched briskly, their swords at the ready. Nobody sought to cross them, although people were everywhere – burying parties, looters and robbers, blood-stained soldiers and wandering priests. But they left them all behind, coming back to the river and following it westward. Ed stumbled wearily behind, wondering what was in store for him. But none of it mattered terribly, without Sigy. He would rather be back a slave with Sigy than a free man without him. And at the thought of Sigy disappearing under the cold spadefuls of earth, Ed wept as he walked, and did not care who saw him.

Chapter 11

Wistan took horses on his way. Ed was given a small, broad beast and learned to ride the hard way, travelling across the breadth of England at the fastest pace possible. Through rivers and forests, over downland, across stony Roman roads and tracks deep in mire – their horses trotted bravely in the wake of the flying king. Cnut and his army followed. Villagers fled at their coming, not knowing peace from war.

When they got to the banks of the river Severn the two kings met to sign the treaty. Not in battle, but in peace with their councillors. Edmund Ironsides was to take the west of the country and Cnut the east. Wistan stood with his king's men at the signing and his brother stayed beside him like his shadow, terrified of losing sight of his only companion in this alien world. He was seeing history made, he understood. The bishops prated and chanted and the two kings knelt before them and repeated oaths over sacred relics. The councillors whispered together and produced parchment treaties which must be signed. Ironsides' hand trembled as the quill scratched. Cnut had not yet learned to write, and laughed. How ill Ironsides looked! Rumour had it he had been wounded in battle, but he would not admit to it. Or was it the sickness of losing half his country to the young Dane that caused his fever?

After the signing he retired to some nearby shelter to prepare to return to his base at Glastonbury. Wistan would go with him.

"You can come too, young Firehead, and make yourself useful at court," Wistan said. "There are rich pickings to be had after battle and all the estates of the dead to be distributed. Ironsides trusts me and I shall be rewarded."

But Ed had only just stopped being a slave. Being promoted to king's company was more than his bewildered brain could accept. He didn't want to be a courtier. He didn't want to be a soldier. He didn't know what he wanted – apart from a warm dry place to roll up in and go to sleep.

The marshy banks of the river Severn were

no more hospitable than the salt marsh at home, and hundreds of both kings' followers had to make camp over the days of the treatying as best they could. It was now the beginning of November and the weather was cold and wet. Wistan's men set up a makeshift sort of tent with poles and skins up above the floodline. Ed was welcome there but felt completely at sea in this company of hardened men talking politics. Shortly they would move on to Glastonbury with the king. Ed had no desire to go.

He missed Sigy as if a part of his body were missing. They had been inseparable for four years, closer than twins. With Sigy Ed could have scoffed at this new way of life, laughed, made plans to do something with their freedom. But without him he was like a leaf blown by the wind.

Now they weren't fighting, the soldiers – of both armies – spent all their time eating and drinking and dropping insensible. There was nothing else to do until they were moved on. Most of them had no home but the army. The recruited ones had already returned home.

Hunched in his cloak, staring at the swift waters of this West Country river beyond the muddy campsite, Ed watched some men taking their horses down to drink. One of the horses was familiar. Ed lifted his head sharply, recognizing the grey stallion he had groomed so often – Rollo's stallion Sky. And the boy leading him. . .

"Rollo!"

He ran. Rollo swung round. His face lit up with pleasure.

"Edmund! I thought you were killed!"

Rollo's pleasure was as genuine as Ed's. They watered the horse and told each other everything that had happened to them since the battle. Rollo had stayed beside Ohtar, and found the life of soldier-cum-courtier as tedious as Ed. Ohtar was bodyguard to Eadric Streona, the traitor who was now one of Cnut's councillors.

"Eadric Streona!" It seemed fitting that Ohtar should join forces with this powerful but hated man.

"Yes. I go along with Ohtar – he's the only person I know. I'm in his camp, where it's all drinking and plotting – who will get what land, what share of the gold, which hostages. . . I'm fed up with it. Ohtar loves it. He makes friends with all the people he thinks will do him good. The king is making Eadric aelderman over Mercia – a reward for betraying Ironsides and winning us the battle – so Ohtar is sucking up to him to get a powerful position and some land of his own. They call him Eadric Streona, the acquisitor, because he grabs so much land. Mostly in lieu of taxes from poor devils who can't pay. I don't want to stay with them. I'd rather go home."

When he said that, Ed felt a strong wrench of nostalgia for the smell of the shore and the sound of crying gulls, his old familiar paths. He could walk them now without anyone telling him what to do.

He thought of Estrid.

"I wouldn't mind going back, now I'm free. But Wistan will stay with the king."

"You could become a thane like Wistan. Wistan is very well-regarded – Cnut thinks highly of him. I heard them talking."

"He's not like Ohtar."

"No."

"Ohtar would have killed me if Wistan hadn't been there."

He told Rollo what had happened.

"It was better Sigy died," Rollo said.

"Yes, but he was dying without Ohtar's help."

Rollo sucked on a blade of grass, thoughtful.

"He's sent word home, you know, that you are dead. To tell Estrid."

"No!"

"He's arranging for Eadric's son to marry her."

"*No!*" Edmund stared at Rollo, horrified.

"Girls always have to marry for what good it does the family. You know that."

If Estrid had been going to marry Cnut, Ed would have accepted it, but Eadric's son! He was a hopeless, spoilt youth with boils on his face and as cowardly in battle as his father. Ohtar obviously cared nothing for his sister.

"She can't marry him! Your father wouldn't want it!"

"To the son of the King of Mercia – of course he would!"

"Your father is kind. I don't think he would."

"Well, it's how it works. My mother married my father without knowing him."

Ed was stunned into silence. He thought of the innocent Estrid, still a child, in the bed of the pimply wimp that was Eadric's son, and shuddered. Yet she would lie in his own arms, he knew. Now he was a free man, brother of Wistan, could he approach her? Get to her before Ohtar finished his evil machinations? Save her from such a dreadful fate?

"Are you going home?" he asked Rollo.

"I don't want to stay here."

"Shall we go together?"

Rollo, lying in the grass chewing a straw, turned over abruptly and sat up.

"What do you mean?"

"Ride together. Wistan will give me a horse. There's nothing here for us."

Rollo's eyes gleamed. "I want to go back to our ship," he said, "and sail with Cnut when he goes back to Denmark. I know he's got to go back soon, to sort out his kingdom since his father died. I don't want to be a warrior – that fighting scared me out of my wits! But I would do anything to be on the ship again. I want to take her round to Lundenburg and join up with Cnut's ships that lie there."

"I would like to find my family. We had no time after the battle, but they are supposed to be in Lundenburg. If they knew Wistan was with the king. . ."

Lying in the grass side by side, they stared up at the now dusking sky. They had never thought of themselves as free men before, not even Rollo, but now it seemed the whole world was waiting for them. They had horses, and gold from the battlefield, and were old enough to follow their own paths. Wistan would give his blessing, Edmund knew, and Ohtar was too busy with his scheming to care about Rollo.

They glanced at each other. Each could see his own excitement in the other's eyes.

"Shall we go?"

"Yes!"

"Now?"

"If we move off tonight, no one will know we're gone. I don't want Ohtar to know I've gone with you."

"Wistan will put him off our track. I'll go and speak to him."

"We'll leave separately, and meet on the road."

Instinctively, they each put out a hand and clasped the other's. Like Ironsides and Cnut, Ed thought, the Saxon and the Dane. Brothers.

But Ohtar was no brother.

Chapter 12

Wistan gave Edmund a good horse, a small black beast, very willing. He gave him a pouchful of gold and small coins which Ed buckled round his waist beneath his tunic. He gave him a fine cloak and a sword from the battlefield, not as beautiful as Ohtar's, but with a shining blade.

"If you wish to find me again, I shall be with the king."

"Don't tell Ohtar I've gone with Rollo. Don't tell him where we've gone."

"No. He's no friend of mine, any more than yours."

"He would have killed me, if you hadn't come that day."

"He's left such a mark on you, Firehead, that I would gladly see him die."

Ed put his hand up to his scored cheek, feeling the width of the scar. But it was paler now, according to Rollo, and – thanks to Sigurd's skill – mending without puckering. He was still handsome enough, he hoped. His hair was growing and the fiery curls would return. Would Estrid still love him? At the thought of her his heart thudded with excitement.

They shook hands in parting, and Ed rode to join Rollo on his faithful Sky.

Rollo said, "Let's ride fast! Ohtar won't be far behind us. He's going to fetch Estrid."

"Fetch Estrid?"

"To take her to Eadric. They want the wedding before Eadric sets himself up in Mercia."

Ed gasped. "So soon!"

"Ohtar's frightened she might be betrothed already. He knows Father's planning. . ." He laughed. "But she's mad for you, Firehead. She'll scream and bite when she hears who she has to marry."

Ed was stunned by Rollo's news. What hope had he got? It was happening too fast for him. Everything, from Sigy's death, to finding Wistan ... his freedom ... he hardly knew where he stood. What had he to offer Estrid, compared with a whole kingdom? He groaned out loud.

"She's a firecat," Rollo said. "You'd be well-suited." He laughed again.

His lithe body turned in the saddle to see how his friend was faring. Rollo had ridden since birth. Ed was reminded of all the parts that ached so cruelly when put across a horse. If only he had taken up Sigy's invitation to ride his beloved Aurelia! He might then look as elegant as Rollo on the prancing stallion. But another two hundred miles might further the improvement. They had no time to lose to keep ahead of Ohtar.

Rollo knew the way no better than Ed, save that it was east into the sun as soon as they rose, and keep it on the right through the day. They rode to Cirencester on the good Roman road, then high over the downs where they could see for miles over forests into the blue distance with the larks and curlews filling the sky with song. And on through Thatcham and Staines, still on the remains of the Roman road, sleeping at night wherever some peasant would accept a coin and find fodder for the horses and a straw pallet.

When they drew near Lundenburg they were told that it was still in a state of siege, not yet knowing what king to welcome, and it would be unwise to try and pass through it. All through the invasions the city had held out, at terrible cost. Ed wondered whether Oswy had fled with the family, or whether they had stayed and suffered the dreadful privations. It might well be hard to find them again. But that task had to wait for a while.

So they rode north at Brentford and went through Tottenham and eventually came on the road they knew, the old Roman road to Colnecaester. Then down along tracks to Maldon and out along the south shore of the river, past the island where the great Byrhtnoth had been slain fifteen years before. Now Ed knew every cow path and hare run and a great love for his own place filled him with excitement. As they came on to the old familiar road to Othona he felt his pulse begin to race. Rollo would get a fine reception, but he, the slave ... where did he belong now? And how far ahead of Ohtar were they? Did Ragnar and his wife even know that Rollo was alive?

They slowed down as they approached the driveway into the settlement. Already the dogs were barking. Smoke plumed up through the roof of the longhouse into the evening sky and there was a smell of meat cooking as well as the old smell of the river and rotting seawrack which Ed knew was home. The slaves were bringing the cows home, replacement slaves that Ed didn't recognize. But Thored was there, his face suddenly alight with recognition.

They slid wearily from their horses and the slaves took them as Ragnar came, startled, out into the last of the evening sun. To Ed he looked really old suddenly, and Ed remembered the crude strength of Ohtar, and knew Ohtar would get his way and push his father aside. But Rollo, the favourite, was embraced with tears.

"No word came! We thought you were dead! Dear Rollo!"

"And Ed too, father. He met his brother Wistan, who is thane to the king."

Ed knelt before Ragnar but Ragnar pulled him to his feet and embraced him too.

"No longer a slave . . . you always had too much will for a slave, eh, Edmund? Edmund Firehead – you were well named. Were you in the battle, the two of you? And Ohtar?"

"Ohtar is on his way home now. We were all in the battle, but unharmed. Only Sigy was killed."

Rollo didn't add, by Ohtar.

Estrid stood behind her mother, very quiet. She was white-faced, looking at Ed. Now that she was older her thick blonde hair was no longer loose but drawn back into a heavy coil at the back of her neck and covered with a gold scarf. Her eyes were very blue, like Rollo's, and very direct, not hiding her feelings. Ed had no need to ask what she felt, glancing at her behind her mother. But the old status of slave in these surroundings was not easy to throw off. For all the gold in his belt and his fine horse he found it difficult to approach the centre of the longhouse to sit at the top of the board with Ragnar and his family. But the mother pressed him, taking his arm, and the slaves were hustled into bringing the best ale, the pigs were chased out and the fire stirred up to cook more meat. As the sun went down outside into a frosty night, the sparks flew up in the smoky roof and the shadows danced over the walls. Ed had to sit beside Ragnar, with Rollo on the other side, like a son. With his back to the hearth the firelight danced round his head, and Estrid's eyes never turned away. Ed dared not meet her gaze – it made him tremble too much.

When they slept, he slept with Rollo on the top bench. The women disappeared behind a curtain. Ed lay awake, his nostrils full of the familiar smell of smoke and roast meat and trodden earth. It seemed a very long time since he had been chained to a post in the hut outside. Yet he thought he would have felt more at home in the old hut, or with the slaves, than he did up here with his gold rings and fine-woven tunic and an embroidered woollen blanket to cover him instead of a stinking goatskin. He was still a peasant boy, in spite of Wistan, yet he had the nerve to covet a princess.

Or, by the look of it, she would claim him, which might make the whole sorry tangle easier. And frighten him to death.

Chapter 13

Ohtar sent a messenger to announce his imminent arrival. His poor little horse was in a lather of sweat.

"Trust Ohtar," Rollo groaned. "He wants us all out cheering and waving a welcome."

"Have you told Estrid his plan for her?" Ed asked anxiously.

"I've told my father. He was very pleased."

Ed glanced across the longhouse to where Estrid and Hilde were giggling over their chores. Estrid had been laughing all morning, casting glances towards Ed. The message he received was as clear as that delivered by Ohtar's advance party. He was keyed up with love and despair.

"I don't think he's told her," Rollo added, unnecessarily.

But even while they watched, Estrid's mother came out of the women's quarters and said something to Estrid. She gestured sharply to Hilde. The two girls stood up abruptly, their giggles halted, and followed the mother back into their quarters. The mother then came out and approached Ragnar who was talking to Thored at the hearth, and spoke seriously to him. Ragnar made a grimace, grinned at Thored, and followed his wife back behind the curtains.

Ed could hear his own heart beating. Rollo pretended indifference, but could not contain his curiosity.

And, as if to satisfy it, a loud scream came from the private quarters, followed by a storm of weeping.

"No! No! No!"

Further shrieks alerted the working slaves from their tasks. Their faces turned in amazement. Ed, feeling sick, heard Rollo snort with laughter beside him.

"I told you! She's a firecat."

The curtains were ripped apart and Estrid hurtled through, both Hilde and her mother clinging on to her arms. She shook them off like a fighting terrier its rats. She turned and faced them, her face bright with fury.

"Don't touch me! I won't do it! I won't! I would rather die!"

Ed thought she looked amazing, all her

golden hair shaken loose and flying, her white tunic swirling round her frenzied body. He stood up, shaking, and she turned and ran towards him. Dogs and hens flew out of her path in a flurry of fur and feathers. She flung herself at Ed, nearly knocking him off his feet. Her slender arms grasped him and the great cloud of her hair filled his face, blinding him, as she pressed her head into the crook of his shoulder.

"Edmund! Edmund, I want to marry *you*!"

"Estrid, you're crazy! Father will have you flogged," Rollo said sharply. "Leave him alone!"

He shoved at her none too gently, prising her grasp from Ed's shoulders. Estrid turned and sank her teeth into his hand. Rollo shouted out and gave her a great swipe round the head, and Hilde came up behind him and kicked him sharply on the ankles.

"How dare you hit my lady!"

Rollo roared with laughter.

"Fighting cat! Do you want her, Ed? If you don't she'll kill you!"

Ed didn't quite know whether he was laughing or crying. The scene confused him utterly – he, so recently a slave, now embracing the jarl's daughter in public. Over the girl's sobbing shoulders he saw all the faces grinning – his erstwhile companions – and, approaching fast, the furious countenance of his benefactor Ragnar.

"Estrid!" Ragnar's voice was like a thunderclap.

Estrid lifted her head. Ed saw her wonderful sky-blue eyes crystal bright with tears – for him – searching his face, and could not resist stroking the wild hair and saying in a voice surely not his own: "It will be all right, Estrid. I will look after you."

"By the god Thor, you are mad!" Rollo hissed at him.

Ragnar reached out and with a steely arm whirled Estrid round to face him. He was as angry as Ed had ever seen.

"Do not use your witchery on poor Edmund! He hasn't asked for your love, you stupid girl. You will do what your father orders, and if you do not obey me we shall have Edmund flogged in front of you until he drops."

At this Estrid screamed out again. Ed stood feeling wildly indignant, as angry with himself as with Ragnar at the mixture of his feelings. He heard Rollo say, "That's rotten, father – Ed's done nothing to encourage her," and the reply, "She will see sense by it, I hope. I mean it."

His eyes flicked angrily at Ed, in that moment looking horribly like Ohtar's. Ed felt his hot blood cooling rapidly.

"Stop making an exhibition of yourself in front of the slaves," he barked at Estrid. "Get back to your quarters. And you two, come to me privately now. We don't want the whole world knowing our business." His curt nod was directed to Rollo and Ed. "Ohtar is only two hours away. We cannot have this disarray when he arrives."

He shouted to Thored and gave a torrent of orders to set the longhouse into celebratory mode, get the fires started and the cooking under way. The slaves all jumped into action, jerked out of their fascination with the behaviour of their master's daughter. They looked at Ed and Ed could see half derision, half admiration in their eyes. Estrid had set him up disastrously. He felt as marked as by the brand Thored had once scorched in his back. That moment felt like a whole world ago, so changed was his fortune, yet it was a mere four years. And, like the brand itching as it often did, the memory of Sigy suddenly returned, bringing hot tears to his eyes. *Sigy!* But in the afterlife perhaps Sigy enjoyed a paradise he had certainly never found on earth. For a moment a touch of envy coloured Ed's thoughts. Ohtar would be arriving shortly and would love Ragnar's scheme for bringing Estrid to heel.

He followed Rollo into the inner sanctum and stood to attention as Ragnar glared at him. He and Rollo, Estrid and Hilde stood in a chastened row before him.

"When Ohtar comes, we shall receive him with dignity and obedience. He has made a marriage contract for Estrid which is of great advantage, to the son of the King of Mercia. No one could seek a higher honour. If you do not receive him kindly, Estrid, I shall punish you in the way I mentioned. I don't want to speak of it again, as it would distress me as much as it would you. But, do not doubt me, I mean what I say."

"Who is this man I am to marry?" Estrid asked boldly. "Is he seventy years old with one leg and squint eyes?"

"No," said Rollo, "he's seventeen and covered in boils and pimples. He's got a receding chin and a large Adam's apple."

"He's the son of a traitor," Ed said chokingly. Even Ragnar could not approve of that.

Estrid's bold chin trembled and tears started to pour down her cheeks.

"Father!" she said imploringly.

Ragnar lost patience. "You are being ridiculous! You know – have always known – that a girl's marriage is a barter arrangement. You cannot plead ignorance! Edmund is no longer a slave, but he has nothing to offer you. Ohtar has done brilliantly to give us this opportunity."

"Ed's brother is thane to the king," Rollo said.

"Silence!" Ragnar roared.

"The king is going to reward my brother for his loyalty with land and estates," Ed added. "He will share it with me."

Even to himself he had to admit that nothing he could offer could compete with the son of the King of Mercia. And Ragnar smiled, knowing it, and said, "I am not arguing with you. The subject is closed. Go and clean yourselves and fetch out the best cask of wine. We have much to celebrate."

Estrid let out a pitiful wail but Ragnar shook her into silence, and her mother and Hilde started to fetch her best clothes and jewels from her trunk to deck her out to meet her betrothed.

"Poor idiot girl," Rollo sighed. "Wait till she sees him!"

Rollo was amused by the whole affair but Ed was shaken to his roots. Rollo said,

"There's nothing you can do about it. I told you. Estrid is being really stupid to put you into such trouble. I think we should leave as soon as possible – take the ship and you come with me. I think Ohtar might kill you otherwise."

Ed had no reason to disagree with Rollo's opinion. All his high – and ridiculous – hopes were dashed. When the wedding was over and Ohtar departed there might still be a home for him here. But without Estrid, without Rollo, the dank shore no longer had much appeal. The events of the last week or two had so thrown him out of dull drudgery – riding free with Rollo across country with money in his belt had been great. Perhaps going on the ship with Rollo would give him fresh ambitions, open up a new way of life. At least it would get him to Lundenburg where he could seek out his family. They could well be in dire straits.

"Come with me," Rollo persisted.

And Ed nodded.

But Ohtar's outriders were approaching and all was excitement in the settlement. Word had gone round that he was bringing Estrid's bridegroom. Great celebrations were about to enliven the grind of work and the mood was merry.

All save for Ed. And what Estrid was feeling – he could only guess. Her fate was far worse than his own.

Chapter 14

Ohtar, riding high on the approval of his king, came home with an arrogance that even Ragnar had forgotten. With young Streona, their bodyguards and hangers-on, he made up a party that Ragnar despaired to accommodate.

Not that Ragnar made any sign.

Ohtar was received as befitted a triumphant son returning to the fold. Ragnar and his wife enfolded him in warm embraces, and offered the same to the pimply youth he had brought with him. If they were disappointed in the figure of the uncouth, ugly boy that was to be their son-in-law, they made no sign. Ed knew that young Streona was as devious as his father, seeing advantage in his friendship with the favoured Ohtar. Ohtar had promised him a beautiful young virgin and he knew he would be extremely lucky to find one elsewhere. Marriages for advantage were usually to old widows. (Even Cnut, it was said, was planning to marry the widow of old King Aethelred, the tired bearer of several children.)

Streona was as far removed in desirability from the straight-backed, green-eyed Fire-head as a lame duck from an eagle. The retainers and slaves all stared in silent grief at Estrid's fate. They had overheard the earlier row. They all loved Estrid, and they liked and respected Firehead. They were not so hardened that they did not recognize the sad story that was being enacted before them.

Ohtar and Streona were ushered into the longhouse where all the best wine and meats were laid out. Everyone ran to serve them. Ed stayed in the shadows away from the hearth, out of sight, but Rollo had to sit beside Ohtar and Streona and look happy. They all ate and drank heavily. When dusk started to fall and the torches were lit along the dishevelled board, it was time for Estrid to make her appearance and be introduced to her bride-groom.

Ed's throat was dry. He had eaten nothing and drunk only a horn of ale. What a fool he had been to come back, thinking he could outwit the powerful Ohtar! Far better not to have witnessed this awful betrothal. He could not even remember why he had set out on this wild-goose chase with the careless Rollo.

Streona, three-quarters drunk, lolled over the table beside the strident Ohtar. Ragnar signalled to one of the women slaves to fetch Estrid.

The mother, stone-faced, came out from the women's place holding Estrid by the hand. Hilde pressed close behind.

Estrid was dressed in white, her cloud of golden hair loose and threaded with coloured ribbons. Jewelled brooches fastened the shoulders of her dress, and her arms were bare and braceletted with gold and silver. Ed had never seen her look so beautiful. Hilde, in sombre grey, looked puffy-eyed with weeping, but Estrid's eyes were glittering bright. They took in the red-faced, grinning Streona like darts to the prey.

Streona had the grace to stand up before her, but he swayed on his feet. Ohtar got up to stand beside him, grinning. Ragnar took Estrid's hand in his.

"This is my daughter Estrid whom I give you in betrothal of marriage with my blessing."

Estrid lowered her eyes.

Ohtar put a rough arm round her shoulders

and said something coarse to Streona, at which Estrid's chin came up. She spat full in Ohtar's face. And with her beringed white hand she hit Streona violently across his face, so hard that he staggered back, tripped over the bench and fell on the floor. Ohtar's dogs turned their muzzles on him with delight.

"Estrid!"

Ragnar struck her in rage. His wife screamed. Hilde screamed. Ed jumped up and without thinking leapt out of his dark corner. Rollo turned and held him fast, hissing, "Keep out of it, you fool!" and the urgency of his voice was enough to make Ed pause. But Ohtar had seen him. Wiping the spittle from his face, he looked incredulous, then almost disfigured with rage.

"Father! I cannot believe this – this – " Words failed him. He had to stop in order to call off his dogs as Streona shouted from the floor. Streona made an undignified recovery, helped by servants. Ohtar kicked the dogs out of the way. Estrid stood white-faced and said, "I will die before I marry him."

Ragnar turned to her and said, "You have disgraced us all. I told you what your punishment would be. I warned you." And to Thored, "Take Edmund."

His words were curt and icy. He looked

crucified at his own action. As soon as he said this Estrid broke into a storm of weeping and turned to her father to put pleading arms round him, but he pushed her away.

"You do not *think*, Estrid! You are a stupid girl. You know I am a man of my word."

Ed's arms were already in the powerful grip of Thored on one side and a massive slave called Rus on the other. He could not believe his bad luck. Yet a mad part of him was exulting at Estrid's wild behaviour. The outrage on Ohtar's face was almost worth dying for.

"Flog me, Father, not Edmund! Please, please, please! You can flog me to death, I would rather! Please, Father! Edmund has done nothing to displease you, not ever! This is all my fault! *Please*, Father."

The mother was now crying silently, and took Estrid in her arms as Ragnar pushed her away.

Ragnar said to Thored, "Take Edmund outside and tie him to the post."

Thored and Rus almost lifted Ed off his feet in their haste to leave the scene. Rollo came with them, muttering angrily.

"The stupid, stupid girl! Is she mad? Why didn't you hide, you idiot? You're almost as stupid – the two of you are well suited! Ohtar will see that you are all but killed – you can bank on that. I'll go back and see if I can argue with Father."

"He's a man of his word, your father. More's the pity," Thored said.

The night air was like spice to Ed's reeling senses. A cold west wind was blowing across the shore. Thored tied his wrists with hide strips and fixed them above his head to the battered old post that had seen many such punishments.

"There's been a lot of wine drunk. Perhaps we can turn the tide, young Firehead. The guv'nor's heart isn't in this job, that's for sure."

Ed knew that there was no hope of the loyal Thored letting him escape, however much he might wish it. He stood in the cold night, knowing that he had come to the end of this particular road. Days recovering in a cold hut was all he had to look forward to, with Estrid gone, and probably Rollo too, in his proud ship. Tears of self-pity sprung to his eyes. The punishment was fearful, and nothing but a gutted life lay ahead of him. Why ever had he left Wistan's side? It was true what Rollo said, he was as stupid as Estrid. He knew that Estrid had not been able to contain her behaviour, just as he could not have stayed in the shadows.

Thored and Rus left him, and only the dogs came and lay down at his feet. He thought that the flogging would be swiftly delivered, but the minutes passed and nobody came. He could see that there was still a fair hubbub going on, and a lot of shouting, but it sounded drunken, and he could not hear Ragnar's voice. As his blood cooled, so his apprehension grew. His hands grew numb and his shoulders ached. He had suffered enough at Ohtar's instigation, one way and another. He nursed to himself the look of disbelief on Ohtar's face. Certainly his homecoming had not been the triumph he had expected! But as the long minutes slipped past Ed's own pain began to over-take the more comforting thoughts. Surely they weren't all going to go to sleep and for-get about him? Was he going to have the whole night to ponder on the flogging to come? He began to feel very cold and shivery.

It was Rollo who came at last. He cut the thongs holding Ed.

"They're all asleep. My father has retired. He said he would see to your punishment in the morning. I think it distresses him – he wants to put it off. He might get Estrid to grovel and be nice to that oaf, and perhaps

you will get off more lightly. I thought..."
He paused.

Ed stood groggily, rubbing his numb wrists. "Thought what? If I make an escape now, you'll probably get flogged instead of me."

"I know that. I just thought – " He considered, hesitant. "The gods are on our side. The tide is high at dawn. We could go as we intended, in the ship, both of us."

"What, tonight?"

"I've been thinking about it. We could take the absolute minimum of men – eight, perhaps. I can easily rouse eight who would come, for their freedom. Assuming we're not caught – but once at sea, who would catch us?"

Ed saw the brilliance of the idea. Even if Ohtar saw them from the shore he would be powerless to stop them. Or chase them. There was only one ship on the river. The little rough fishing coracles would never catch a Norseman's ship. It was a fine idea.

"I could wake eight men from the outside huts. No one would see us. They could collect enough food from the table. If anyone sees them they'll just think it's the usual slave stealing – they won't bother. There's a fair wind – we could sail straight out of the river and be out of sight by daylight. Get to Lundenberg and Ohtar will never find you."

Ed had never thought he would feel so keen to go sailing. His cold blood started to move.

"I'll do all that's necessary," Rollo said. "You go down to the ship and undo the warps. Just leave one to hold her. She'll be aground until an hour before high water – we'll be with you by then. It's best you're out of here, in case anyone awakes. The dogs might start barking if we're unlucky."

But the dogs knew all the slaves.

"I'll try and rouse sailing men, not pigherders. I know the best ones. You go now. If something goes wrong – well at least, you're free. I'll take the blame for letting you go."

"What about – "

Ed was going to say, "What about Estrid?" but decided that Rollo couldn't care less about Estrid. It was she who had got them into this mess. *He* cared about her – that was something different. But he was powerless to help her. He must make the best of it. If she married Streona – well, perhaps Streona would die or get killed. There could well be another day.

Rollo's plan was brilliant. Not having been keen to sail, Ed was now as keen as Rollo. To escape the looming punishment now became his most ardent ambition. With luck they would get away unseen. After such high emotions – and heavy drinking – sleep would be sound in the settlement. No one in the longhouse would rise early. Ed shrugged his stiff shoulders and set off for the river. On the way out he collected an armful of sheepskins that might come in useful. He dared not go back into the longhouse for his cloak.

But Rollo had been bolder. When he came back with a posse of men they carried blankets, food and a cask of ale.

"There was no danger," Rollo said. "They sleep like the dead."

Even in the darkness Ed could sense Rollo's excitement. Everything that had happened in the longhouse meant little to him – nothing compared with taking the ship out to sea. This was his life's ambition. His voice trembled with excitement.

And now Ed saw that the danger was by no means over. If they failed and were caught then the punishments all round would be terrible. The slaves were clearly nervous, dying to get away. They did not look like the seasoned sailors Ed had expected – more the younger men that did the most menial tasks. They slept in the outside huts and had been easy to rouse. Ed had no idea what future

Rollo had promised them. At that moment he did not much care. His own future was of more concern.

A cold wind blew but it was fair. They could use the sail to get away. The ship was aground, but the tide was rising fast and soon she would lift. The heavy warps dipped and swung in the water and snubbed the ship's impatience. It was a cloudy night but the hidden moon still gave a fair light and cast a leaden sheen over the estuary. Dawn was not far away. A cock crew in the distance, and was answered from far away down the shore. Ed felt his skin prickle with a strange nostalgia for this home that he was leaving again.

"Get the sail unloosed," Rollo shouted at him.

He was galvanized into action as the great wooden craft at last shook herself free of the holding ground. The last warp that held her stretched suddenly tight. The men started to pole her off with the long oars.

Ed ran forward to the mast and tore at the knots that held the sail furled. Two men hauled down on the halyard and the huge stiff sail cracked free with a life of its own. Rollo stood at the steering-board, tugging the tiller backwards and forwards to free it from the mud.

"She's going!" someone shouted.

The sail seemed to blot out the whole sky. Ed felt the heavy boards creak and move beneath him. It was as if a huge slumbering animal was awaking from a long sleep, stretching its limbs with renewed strength. The ship shuddered with joy, meeting the first wave and throwing a fine spray over them all.

And just as the ship took off they all heard shrill screams from the shore. Something white moved there, screaming.

"Take me! Take me!"

Over the cracking of the unbending sail the voice came clear as a gull's cry, piercing in its desperation. Ed's heart came into his mouth.

"Estrid! The crackpot!" Rollo cried.

Estrid screamed at them again, and even as they watched the white shape disappeared from sight.

"By the gods, she'll drown!" Rollo cried. "She's swimming out."

Ed stood frozen with horror. He could see now the two girls – Hilde as well – clear of the muddy saltings, striking out into the deep water. It was a hopeless attempt to catch the ship, for with the wind in her sail she was now moving faster and faster down the river, faster than ever the girls could swim.

"They'll drown!" Ed's voice cracked.

But Rollo shouted, "Let down the sail! Let go the halyard!"

Ed leapt to obey. The sail crashed down all over him, as Rollo put the tiller over and brought the ship round to face the shore again. But the wind carried her sideways even without the sail. The girls could be seen bobbing in the water, making no progress against the tide that held them back.

Rollo shouted at the men. "Who can swim? We'll bring the ship back to you, never fear! I swear to you – if you fetch them safely – you will be rewarded! I swear by my life!" His voice cracked.

Ed moved forward. Rollo snatched his arm.

"Not you. Stay here. I need you." His voice was just like Ragnar's and as commanding.

But Ed was no longer a slave. He pulled himself free, launched himself up on the gunwale and jumped.

He heard Rollo scream at him, furious.

Ed, until now, had thought he could swim. But the quenching iciness of the water and the panic for Estrid in his stomach was more than a match for his enthusiasm. The sea hit him like a cliff, hard and hostile. It took his breath, his sight, his senses. What had he done? He was drowning himself, let alone Estrid.

He shouted out. Floundered. Sank. But

there was bottom under his feet. He felt ground, pushed off, saw the great bows of the ship looming above him. There were more men in the water all round him, a white face looming alongside, shouting at him.

"Call that swimming?" A laugh and a grin.

Ed, galled, struggled to half swim, half stride towards the white blur he could now make out against the shore. But the ground beneath his feet was such a relief that his panic faded. He could laugh too. His love for Estrid, for her crazy bravery, set his blood alight. He shouted, "Estrid! Estrid!"

The man beside him said, "That's right – wake Thored! You'll have them all awake and out on the shore."

But it was into his arms that Estrid floundered, laughing, crying, her hair in great wet ropes round his face. The men bore her up, and Hilde with her, and Ed held her and got swept back to the ship in the mêlée. Rough arms grabbed them from above. But the ship was aground and they had to jump back and push her bows round, back out facing the sea. It was touch and go, the tide on the turn, the first pale streak of dawn already softly washing the eastern sky.

The rest of the crew poled frantically. They were all terrified now that the ship was beached. Their lives depended on their wild efforts. The yellow streak of dawn was growing longer across the beckoning horizon, spurring their desperation.

"She's free!"

Rollo screamed at the men to go on poling the bows to make the ship come round. Ed got hauled aboard and ran to the halyard to haul mightily on the sail. The great rough folds of canvas flogged wildly in the wind. Another man came to help, and the swimmers clambered frantically back on board as the great lumbering ship shook herself free. It was as if she too had had enough of the shore. As the sail blossomed out and filled she dipped and rose and picked up speed. In the grey light the strained faces broke into smiles and laughter and when one man let out a cheer it was picked up by the others. Even Rollo was laughing, standing proudly on the steering-board platform. Ed remembered his first sight of him just like that – it seemed a lifetime ago.

"There's no going back now – it won't only be you slaves that will be punished!" he shouted happily. "All of us!" He laughed.

And to Ed, softly, "You're a madman! Well-named Firehead – you can't swim, can you?"

"I thought I could!"

"We truly are in deep water now. Just us – no loss, really. But now Estrid is with us, Ohtar will scour the sea and the land from here to Siberia to find us. Where are we going to make landfall?"

And to that there was no answer.

Chapter 15

It was the gods who decided where the ship went.

Rollo thought Colnecaester, to the North, where Ohtar was unlikely to find them, but when the ship reached out of the river and into the German ocean a northerly wind blew up which it was impossible to drive into. The ship must turn south and run with the wind. They stood far out but Ohtar, with his hawk's eyes, could well see them from the Othona shore. The visibility was bright and clear. It was very cold.

Ed visualized Ohtar gathering his henchmen around him and setting out along the coast to try and keep the ship in sight.

"He knows we want to go into the Thames," Rollo said to Ed. "But we'll sail on south and put you off on the Kentish shore. He will never reach you there. Then you must find Wistan."

Where was Wistan? Ed knew that he could only be safe from Ohtar under Wistan's wing. There was no hope for him otherwise. As far as he knew Wistan was still in Glastonbury.

Rollo assumed that Ed would take Estrid and Hilde with him. Ed's fires of love were cooled by the prospect. What did he know about girls, for Heaven's sake? He only knew about love from a distance, watching and fantasizing, egged on by Estrid's glances and blushes. He knew nothing of how to keep girls safe, how to keep them warm and fed in an unknown territory, how to travel with them – being responsible! A slave nearly all his recent life, he now had to take command. He was not used to ordering men, let alone girls. Weighed by his doubts, he kept silent. He rowed at one of the oars, trying to find courage. This was what he wanted, wasn't it? Estrid was delivered from Streona. She loved him. She would follow him even into danger.

The girls slept under the furs while their wet clothes were hung out in the wind to dry. The ship rolled and plunged in the choppy waters of the great estuary of the Thames. She was travelling athwart the tide, moving farther and farther from the flat Essex shore and out of Ohtar's sight. But dangerous shoals lay all around them. Rollo had a man in the bows swinging a leadline to check the depth of water. With every mile they sailed Ed felt his heart lifting, free of the threat of Ohtar's sword. Yet new fears crowded in – Kent was a foreign land to Ed, as good as France. He was scared, excited. He had escaped being flogged almost to death, he had won Estrid, he had beaten Ohtar, yet now he could only think of the responsibilities that lay ahead. Was a man never content!

Gradually in the thin autumn sunshine a blue shore began to emerge on the horizon, growing slowly sharper and more distinct as the heavy sail dipped and filled to the north wind.

"We are lucky to make such a good passage," Rollo laughed. "Ohtar will never reach you here."

"Land us on a deserted shore. We don't want a deputation to meet us!"

"There are no enemies here," Rollo said.

Maybe, Ed thought. But they did not want to be noticed or reported. The ship was strange enough as it was, coming in to shore. Ed just hoped that the Kentish shoremen were used to seeing longships hastening up and down their stretch of sea. This was a main artery going up to Lundenberg, not a backwater like the shore he came from. Even now they could see two more ships in the distance, not longships but bulky traders wallowing in the rough water. With luck not too much notice would be taken of their visit.

But Rollo decided to take in sail and slow the ship down.

"We'll sail along the coast until it's dark and land you nearer Lundenberg. No one will see you."

Cnut's ships lay on the opposite – Essex – shore. Rollo would have to make back to join up with them.

"If Ohtar meets up with me," Rollo said, "I'll tell him you landed on the Essex shore. I'll not tell him Kent."

Ed knew he would have to travel to Lundenberg, for only there would he find out where Wistan was, where the king was. No good travelling to Glastonbury if Wistan was on his way to Lundenberg. Perhaps he could find a safe house where Estrid and Hilde could lie up. He thought then of Oswy and his family. Perhaps they were still to be found at their uncle's place, by the Walbrook stream. Oswy could guard Estrid while he went to seek Wistan.

The Kentish shore was broken by inlets and islands. Rollo had a rough chart and knew where he was. Ed was impressed. Such book work was beyond his comprehension. Rollo had not spent his time idly in the settlement.

"We'll land you here, where the river goes up to Rochester. You'll be clear of most of the marshes and can take the Roman road from Canterbury to Lundenberg. It's busy and you can get horses. Perhaps we'll lie here a little while, until Ohtar gives up his search."

Ed wanted to land in the dark, not to be noticed. Rollo agreed it was better, although the night was very cold. He asked Estrid if she wanted to go with Edmund.

"You can come back with us if you wish. Apologize to Ohtar, marry Streona, if you've changed your mind."

Ed would not have been surprised if Estrid had given way. It was warm in the shelter on the ship, where a fire burned low and the men were gathering round to cook a meal. If they landed there was nothing but hardship and uncertainty.

"I will go with Edmund," Estrid said without hesitation.

Ed laughed. A sudden fount of joy broke in him, remembering Sigy, seeing Ohtar's rage. Trouncing Ohtar, denying him his glory – that was worth a kingdom! If he could win through now – what a splendid future lay before him! Estrid his prize, and Wistan his protector – his doubts and fears spun away with the sparks from the fire.

The girls dressed again in their nest under the fleeces, and when the bows of the longship softly ran on to the dark shore, the men carried them on to firm land. Ed followed, carrying a bundle of provisions. Rollo embraced him.

"Your gods guard you, Edmund." His voice choked.

"And you, Rollo."

In his excitement Ed had overlooked the pain of parting from Rollo. It was a stab to his spirits, bringing tears to his eyes. First Sigy, now Rollo. It was likely their paths would not cross again.

He had no words to express his emotion. In the firelight he saw Rollo's face, recognized his own feelings there, and turned away abruptly. He jumped out over the side of the ship, turning his back on what now seemed like a whole chapter of his life – the book closing, his future as unknowable as this foreign Kentish land.

But at least he was well clear of Ohtar. For now.

He did not look back.

Chapter 16

The sky was full of stars, the air frosty. Rolled in the skins they had brought, Ed and the girls slept heavily in a thick copse by the shore. The girls slept first and Ed lay listening to their soft breathing beside him. Estrid's body was pressed close, her arm round his chest, her face turned to his. Under the cave made by the skin she had kissed his face, his scars, his lips, laughing. Laughing! "I am so happy! I love you, I love you, Edmund, and now we are together!" She had no fear. "I love you so much!" Her hand caressed his newly-growing hair, stroked his cheek, his neck. He lay silently, too astounded, too aroused, to scarcely dare breathe, let alone move. What a lover! The shock of events, the flood of emotions, stunned him. And then, like a child, she slept, smiling in the darkness. Ed lay shivering, trembling — he did not know which —

but his own smile kept breaking too, he could feel it, stretching the sore scars, out of his control. The moon came out and shone like a blessing over the black ground. Ed wanted to get up and dance and shout, but kept himself lying there, shaking with this strange ecstasy – whether of love, or fear, or fear of love, he was never to know. Life had never treated him like this before.

The cold light of day banished their fancies. They were starving and frozen. They gathered up their bundle of belongings and stamped inland along a frozen cow track. Out to sea there was no sign of Rollo's longship, only a grey tide rolling back to leave a greyer shore, and a darker line that was Essex scoring the horizon. Was Ohtar riding there, searching for them? Once more the thought of Ohtar's rage buoyed Ed's spirits.

They found a farmer milking who gave them a horn of warm milk each, straight from the cow, and told them where the road lay. On the road were homes and travellers, and Ed had his pouch of coins to buy more food and beds when night came. On such a road they caused no curiosity – it was one of the country's main arteries, with travellers far more foreign than themselves a commonplace.

In two days' walking they reached the road into Southwark where the Thames was bridged – the bridge that Cnut had never breached for all his efforts. It was an impressive thing, patched up from the old Roman structure with great wooden piers. The river was wide and marshy, but wharves had been built on the Lundenburg bank – on the far side – below the bridge. Several ships were berthed there that had come across the German Ocean. These were not fighting ships but trading ships, bulkier and slower, with foreign crews. A few sheds stood on the shore and beyond they could see homesteads with fields adjoining, and pigsties and cowsheds and vegetable patches all strung together along a road leading inland.

On the south side where they stood there was nothing but an unsavoury rabble of poor fishermen's hovels, no place to linger.

Yet Ed was frightened of going into Lundenburg.

"Ohtar will be looking for us there."

"It's you who must stay hidden," Estrid pointed out. "He won't kill *me*."

"He might not kill you, but he will take you," Ed pointed out. "If he sees you, you stand no chance."

"I shall scream and kick and bite – he will not dare!"

She certainly had spirit. She was no soft and nervous girl. The journey had been hard and the living rough, but the girls had laughed all the way and Ed had found the expected burden of caring for them non-existent. They could care for themselves. He had no experience of girls – were they all like that? He had no idea.

"We have no choice," Estrid pointed out. "We can't stay here."

Ed saw the sense of that. Estrid made him wrap a woollen shawl round his head and over his cheeks to hide his hair and scars.

"We'll say you're ill with toothache, and find a place to lie up."

They crossed the bridge and walked along the road that led up from the river till they came to a crossroads where it was much busier. The houses were closer together and workshops and stalls gave on to the street, selling everything from meat to jewellery, leather bags, earthenware jars, shoes, clothes, necklaces... The girls stared, enthralled. Ed, muffled up to the ears, could not get them to move. They lifted up the jewels, their eyes sparkling, fingered the silk and brocade, holding it out to each other. "How much?"

166

they asked the eager stallholders. Ed stood behind them cursing.

"For God's sake, we must find a hiding-place," he muttered at them.

"It's so busy here, we don't show up," Estrid scoffed.

It was true. Ed had never seen so many people (away from battle) shouting and jostling. Horses passed by, splashing up the mud, ridden by haughty merchants, and ox-carts laden with vegetables and timber lumbered heavily in their wake. The girls had found a stall selling bolts of woollen dress-cloth.

"Look at the fineness of it! So soft! And this lovely colour!"

Behind the stall, across a patch of ground given over to a flock of geese, a decent-looking longhouse stood, with a woman in the doorway shaking out some scraps to the birds. Ed told Estrid to ask her if she could give them shelter. They might be safer in the thick of things, and there seemed to be no way of dragging the girls away from this street of delectable objects.

Estrid was only too thrilled to be based in the shopping centre of the capital of England and quickly negotiated a deal with the householder. She had the way of a woman used to giving orders, to go with her upbringing. The householder saw the flash of coins in Ed's moneybag and quickly agreed. Ed put on his ill man's act, and was led to a bench near the central fire and plied with mulled ale. He took care not to show his bright hair, but it was hard to hide the scars and drink at the same time. Hilde went out and came back with a woven cap, which she pulled down over his ears.

"You can buy anything here! It's paradise!"

"If you go out, hide your face too! You must be on the look-out."

"Of course. Don't worry. We know what we're doing."

With that Ed had to be content. He hoped that, when the excitement wore off, he could get them settled and start looking for Oswy. Luckily after the long hike they were tired by afternoon and came back to the bench by the fire, exhausted by the excitements in Westcheap and Eastcheap. The three of them slept then, comfortable at last, and well-fed by the woman who saw profit in these monied strangers. The city was always full of strangers. She was used to it.

In the morning, when Ed made tentative enquiries about the whereabouts of the king, he was told that Ironsides was dead.

"They say he was wounded in battle, and

has been sinking the last week. A messenger came yesterday, from Glastonbury. Straight from the funeral he was, or so he made out."

Ed recalled the trembling hand that signed the treaty. So now Cnut was king of the whole country. Where did that leave Wistan?

"What will happen now?"

"They say Cnut is on his way here. A fine thing – we've spent all these last months under siege from his ships, we never gave in, never, and a terrible hard time we had of it. Now, with Ironsides gone, we must take this man as king, and give him what he never managed to take by fighting."

"He's a friend now. He made peace with Ironsides."

"Perhaps. He'll be coming for his taxes, no doubt. Those Danes have bled us dry over the years."

It was a shock to realize that the country had capitulated at last, and was now to be ruled by an invader. During centuries of fighting the invaders had never conquered the whole country. Now, by dying, Edmund Ironsides had given them what they had so long desired. But Ed respected Cnut. He thought of him as a hero figure with his bravery in battle, his youth and fine looks. He was just yet strong. True, he was cruel and cut off hands and noses, but even quiet Aethelred had set a church on fire and burned to death two hundred innocent people, including Sven Forkbeard's sister. Kings gained power by terror. It was a fact of life.

Ed decided to go looking for Oswy. The city was a large sprawl of homesteads and farms, an overgrown village, but with signs of wealth, finer buildings and smarter people. It seemed to have spread west a good way beyond the Roman walls which still stood where they had guarded the original Roman city. Ruins of Roman buildings lay tumbled in the fields, overgrown with ivy and brush, with trees growing through the stone rubble. The Saxons had just built round them, using their usual materials – timber filled with clay and wattle.

In spite of the recent siege, there was a feeling of vigour and enthusiasm in the air. Rested now, Ed was stirred like the girls by the life and bustle. He had never been in a town before. Horses were being shod, meat butchered; ladies were buying beautiful silk cloth from faraway lands and there was a stall selling beakers of fine blue glass which the stallholder said came from Venice. Ed had no idea where Venice was. He had never seen glass before.

He felt a real country bumpkin, in spite of having rubbed shoulders with kings.

"I love this place," Estrid exclaimed. "I never knew there were such things! Have you seen the brooches the goldsmith is making? All set with rubies! How much money have you brought with you, Edmund?"

"Not enough for gold brooches! It's for our board and lodging until we find Wistan. I'm going out to see if I can find the king's quarters – find out where he will be coming to, and when. We need to know all the news. But you must stay here and lie low. Ohtar is bound to come into town when he can't find us anywhere else. You mustn't be seen!"

"No, we'll see him first! I know how it matters – I don't want to marry Streona! We promise we'll be like mice, Edmund. And you too – you must be careful – cover your face – "

"Don't leave this place, whatever you do." He spoke sternly.

"No, Edmund."

But their eyes danced and he could not believe they would sit dully in the hut waiting for him.

"If you love me, Estrid, don't get seen!"

What else could he say? Catching the old shawl round his face, he hurried away from the distractions of Cheapside to find the royal precinct. Cnut would hardly be coming to Cheapside. Somewhere there was a building fit for a king.

He found it at Aldermanbury, close by the gate to the north called Cripplegate. Banners flew from the roof, horses were stabled nearby, and rather scruffy-looking soldiers in leather jerkins sat round braziers in the cold morning. From them he learned that yes, Edmund had died, and Cnut was said to be on his way. A soldier told him that a party had set out to meet him and would send back fast messengers to prepare for his entry into his capital.

"Thank God!" Ed knew his luck was in. Even if Wistan wasn't with the king, some-body would have news of him.

"It's a fine thing, making welcome for the man we've been fighting all these years," the soldier said disgustedly.

"He's said to be fair. And brave," Ed said.

"He can't be worse than the old king, I dare say. There was a man who never knew his own mind! Pity his son was struck down. He knew more about soldiering at twenty than his father ever learned in fifty years."

Ed listened to the grumbles, feeling at home in this company after his stay with Wistan's men by the Severn river. Whoever fed them, they followed and fought for. It was a rootless life. Yet here in Aldermanbury they were as comfortable as they were ever likely to be. The old Roman wall buildings were still strong and weatherproof and made better shelter than the makeshift hovels and tents he remembered by the Severn. The smell of wood-smoke and cooking meat was homely. He stayed talking for some time. It was good to be with men again. He had been a soldier, after all. When they knew he had fought at Assunden he was accepted as one of their own and offered food. He did not say whose side he had been on. He sat by the brazier gnawing a chicken bone, listening to tall tales of battle, until suddenly the man opposite stood up abruptly.

"Look to yourselves!"

Ed turned round and saw a group of soldiers coming towards them. It was the horse he recognized, Moonfleet ... he had groomed him often enough. Glancing up, he saw Ohtar astride, and young Streona at his side, and their impressive bodyguard filling the street behind.

He had his cap well pulled down but his face was bare with gnawing the chicken bones. Ohtar's glance went over him, looking for authority. Ed froze, not knowing whether to stay or make a run for it. The scars were as good as a brand. His pulses were racing now with fear. He bent down as if searching for a coin in the mud, but even this made him stand out as all the soldiers looked to do Ohtar's bidding.

"You!"

Ed heard the doubt – excitement – in Ohtar's voice.

"With the cap!"

Ed ran.

"Catch that man!" Ohtar roared.

He was saved by the soldiers knowing – hating – Ohtar and having taken a liking to him in the last half-hour, so the chase scarcely got under way. But Ohtar swung the agile Moonfleet round and came after him with screams and bellows. He was beside himself with his ungovernable rage. No doubt he had his sword unsheathed but Ed had no time to look. The city streets were the saving of him, for Moonfleet was unable to twist and turn through the shacks and stalls like Ed could. When Ohtar tried to follow, Moonfleet upset a cart of vegetables and the street people shouted angrily at Ohtar, letting Ed through. Ohtar was screaming out that he would pay well for Ed's capture, but the Lundenburgers knew he was Cnut's man – his voice gave him away. They would not betray him to the likes of Ohtar.

"Get in here, lad!"

A man snatched his arm and pulled him into a doorway.

"Under the fleeces. Lie still."

The bodyguards came searching but had no authority to upturn domestic dwellings. They stood in the doorway, and found hostile eyes on every threshold. Ohtar's exhortations were to no avail. Ed lay like a stone, hardly daring to breathe. His heart was pounding so loudly in his own ears he felt sure they must hear it.

"You've a stout enemy there, mate. What've you done to annoy him?"

The householder came back when the shouts had receded.

"I was his slave," Ed muttered.

"You must have been a damned good one, that he wants you back so badly!" The man laughed. "Rest here till it's safe. No man should be a slave to the enemy."

Ed was terrified that Estrid and Hilde would now be strolling among the stalls in Eastcheap. When Ohtar gave up the chase for him he would turn to searching for the girls. He would guess his sister was not far away. Estrid and Hilde had promised to stay hidden but Ed did not trust them an inch, with such goodies tempting their hearts outside the door. He remembered their dancing eyes. The daft girls only thought of shopping. He must get back and warn them. They must all lie like hibernating hedgehogs until Cnut came to town and Ohtar was distracted. Ohtar would be the first to meet the new king, fawning and looking for favours. Only then would they stand a chance to move. But how to contact Wistan? Ed groaned with the burden of his cares. Only an hour ago he had been really enjoying himself, talking battle. Now he began to wish he had taken Rollo's offer to be a sailor.

He did not dare move out, but with a cheap coin he persuaded the householder's boy to take a message to ... where?

"By a forge, a house standing back, a flock of geese in front. A stall with woollen cloth nearby. You know it?"

The boy nodded.

"Tell the young ladies there on no account to go out of the house. Ohtar is here and looking for them."

"Ohtar?"

"Ohtar. They will understand."

It was the best he could do. He would try and get back to them when it got dark. He sat fretting by the friendly man's hearth. The boy came back and said he had delivered the message to the lady of the house. So Ed didn't know whether the girls were in or out. He kept imagining going back and finding them missing.

The day dragged away into darkness at last and he slipped out and made his way back, losing his way several times. He remembered that he had intended to look for Oswy. His help could be useful. But whether he was still in the city, or had left long ago, he had no way of knowing.

"Estrid?"

To his immense relief the girls were in the house. A domestic scene met his eyes, Estrid plucking a chicken and Hilde playing with one of the little girls. They jumped up when he came in, their eyes lighting up.

"Ohtar chased you!"

"Yes! He'll be scouring the city for us now – you too! We've got to lie low."

"We're safe here. The lady is kind. We've told her the danger we're in."

"I hope she doesn't gossip."

"No. She likes the money, we're safe."

Estrid could not conceal her privileged upbringing and her natural authority made their hosts eager to please. They made them a place well-hidden from the door by some wine barrels, and after supper the three lay there wrapped in fleeces, drifting into sleep. Estrid's hair was in Edmund's face, her arm across his chest. Danger seemed to bring them closer than love alone. Edmund thought he could die for her, looking at her white face resting on his shoulder. Then he thought of his new freedom, the strong figure of his brother Wistan offering him riches and privilege, the whole world ahead of him... No, he did not want to die! And he groaned and pressed his nose into the girl's musky-smelling hair, longing for night to be over and light to come to his muddled senses.

Chapter 17

Cnut rode into the city with a large retinue.
No longer haggard and war-weary, he came in
triumph, with banners and trumpets and
outriders. Most of the occupants of the city
turned out to greet him – or, if not to greet
him, to look curiously on this young man who
had plagued them for so long.

Ed knew it would be wiser to stay away, but
he had to find Wistan. Ohtar would have
more urgent matters to attend to now Cnut
had arrived – with luck, he would have post-
poned worrying about his sister and her
affairs. The city was so crowded suddenly Ed
thought he might venture out again in his
toothache gear. Estrid and Hilde clamoured
to come, but he was sharp with them in his
anxiety.

"No! It's too dangerous!"

"Ohtar will be too busy bowing and

scraping to King Cnut to see us!" Estrid complained.

"So he might. But we'll not risk it. I'll go alone."

He muffled himself up as best he could. Luckily it was very cold and scarves and shawls did not come amiss. He affected a bad limp and hunched his shoulders, crouched into a smelly cloak borrowed from his host. Well-hidden in the crowd, he saw Eadric Streona ride out to greet Cnut with his young son and Ohtar by his side. A clutch of aeldermen, thanes, bishops and clergy milled about the street, waiting to seek favour, and in the crush Ed found it hard to see the men who rode with Cnut. He only saw helmets bobbing and the banners. The crowd was so great, come to see the new king, that in its wash he felt safe enough. But bare his head and show his face, and he did not doubt that Ohtar would pick him out. The glorious sword would finish him off in some far corner of a dilapidated pigsty or crumbling Roman ruin, and his bright future would be put out before it was begun.

The king and his followers disappeared into the fine rooms made ready for them and the crowd started to wander off to make its own celebration. Fires were lit in the fields and cooking and drinking started in earnest. No one was going back to work. Ed wanted to go and talk to the newly arrived soldiers to enquire after Wistan, but dared not. Ohtar's bodyguard were still outside, mingling uneasily with the guards at the gate.

He went back to the girls, trying to work out a way of getting a message to Wistan. But who to ask?

Hilde said, "I could go and look for Wistan. Ohtar won't recognize me."

Ed stared at her. She was right. He hardly recognized her himself, so brown and dirty had she become.

"But you don't know Wistan."

"I can ask," Hilde said. "I've a tongue in my head."

"Ask a soldier. Yes. Go back to Cripplegate and find a man who rode in with Cnut."

"Go quickly," Estrid said. "For soon they'll all be drunk."

Hilde ran. She was like Sigy, Ed thought suddenly, always laughing at authority. If only Sigy were still with him – the burden of guarding Estrid would be halved. But now he was alone with her in the smoky hovel he did not know how to contain her impatience. She was wild to be outside amongst all the excitement. They quarrelled.

"You'd be better chained to the roof post!"

Ed cried out. "Do you want to be found out?"

"No. I want to stay with you."

"If Ohtar finds you, then he will kill me, and that will be the end of what you want. If you want jewels – " he lifted up the frayed end of his tunic belt and held out the little gold heart she had given him, still sewn into the material – "you can have this."

"Edmund!"

"I've always kept it, all this time."

"You do love me?"

She took the heart and lifted it up and kissed it. Then she leaned forward and kissed Ed's cheeks, where the scars were.

"It makes no difference, what Ohtar did. Even if he cut your nose off, I would love you."

"When we are free, I will buy you jewels, I promise."

"And marry me?"

"Yes," he said.

After that she stopped fretting to go outside, and helped the woman cut vegetables and prepare meat for the stewpot, and played with the children. Ed stood at the door of the longhouse, his heart thumping with fear, love and frustration all mixed together. Estrid had a calm about her in the face of danger that impressed him. She was a very certain girl, not at all a frightened mouse, or she would never have come. He wasn't sure that he deserved her, for all her talk of loving him.

But Hilde came back at dusk and said Wistan was there. The relief rolled over Ed like a warm cloak, and he felt the dreadful burden lift.

"Did you see him?"

"How could I? He is one of Cnut's bodyguard, sitting with him, with all the aeldermen and the bishops. I asked a soldier and he pointed out a man called Fric, who he said was Wistan's man. So I spoke with Fric."

"I remember Fric! Did he promise – ?"

"Yes. He said he would tell Wistan where we are when the feast is over."

As long as Fric could be trusted... Ed thought he could, remembering the stocky, cheerful youth.

There was nothing to be done now but wait. The woman served out a good supper and her husband went off drinking, the children slept and they sat round the hearth listening to the distant sounds of revelry. The sky was lit with myriad fires and the smell of roasting meat sweetly drowned the usual smell of the midden, the mud, the cesspit and the marsh. There was frost on the ground and the sky was bright with stars.

"It's a good start for a new king," the woman said, "that he comes in peace. And the night is fine."

Perhaps it would be a new start for him too, Ed thought, weary with his travelling and fear of violence. The city grew quiet just before dawn, and men lay drunkenly by the remains of their fires and the unmilked cows lowed mournfully. The grass stood stiff with frost and footsteps scrunched, rasping in the stillness. Ed heard, and froze. He had no weapon, no defence.

"Edmund?"

A figure darkened the doorway. Ed sat up.

"Is this the right place? Edmund Firehead?"

"Who is it? Wistan?"

"Aelfric. Sent by Wistan."

Ed scrambled to his feet.

"Here. Come in. What is the message?"

Aelfric tiptoed through the doorway and came and squatted down by Ed.

"Wistan says you are in great danger. From Ohtar."

"I know that already."

"He thinks you should go, now, before dawn. There will be a late awakening tomorrow and many thick heads, which will give us a good start."

"Us?"

"I am to take you. We go by boat, up the river. Wistan has sent you money, and a sword, and there is a boat waiting by the bridge. King Edmund left Wistan three estates. One is near the river, at Wanetage – that's where we make for. And wait for Wistan to join us."

Ed couldn't believe it – to have the terrible responsibility lifted from his shoulders! A place to go to, and the resourceful Aelfric to help him! Wistan was a magician. He woke the girls, shaking them, and told them to hurry. The woman woke up and Ed spun her a tale and gave her some money with which she was well pleased.

"If anyone comes asking, you've never set eyes on us, remember."

"No, my dear boy. I never have, on my heart I swear it."

Nothing stirred in the cold night. The girls shivered, pulling their thick cloaks close. Ed realized how fine the plan was. Ohtar had faster horses than they could ever hire, and would not think of the river. With Aelfric to help him and, with luck, a fair wind in the sail, they would slip away deep into the countryside.

"Ohtar's asked everywhere for you," Aelfric told them. "A firehead with scars on his cheeks. We've only been here a day and we know all about it. He'll be watching Wistan like a hawk, but never know his bird has flown."

They came down to the river, seeing no one, and found a boat pulled up by the end of the road with oars laid ready. It was built of wood with a mast and sail. But no wind stirred. The water ran black and quiet, the tide still making, which would help them on their way. The girls got in and huddled in the bottom of the boat, and the two boys pushed the craft out and hopped in. A dog barked but no one answered it. As they rowed away it went on barking after them, its voice echoing across the water. And as it faded, there was only the sound of the dipping oars and grunting breath and, far away, the sad calling of seabirds fishing along the waterline. The boat slipped along easily. The stars faded and behind them in the east the sky started to lighten.

Chapter 18

"You have to enter like a king," Aelfric said. "The place is yours. Wistan's at least. No difference."

Ed did not feel like a king after three days' travelling, first in the boat and then on foot. They stood on the old Roman road along the hilltop and looked down at the fields below. A river looped through the valley and on either side the fields were full of cattle and pigs. Wistan's settlement was well built, tidy and impressive.

"It belonged to a man killed at Assunden. His son was killed too and Ironsides gave it to Wistan in recognition of his courage and loyalty."

"Loyalty? But now he's Cnut's man."

"Only from choice. When Ironsides died Cnut asked him to come to his court. Where else was there to go for a soldier like Wistan?

We are lucky that it was Cnut that conquered us, and not a bloodthirsty pagan like his father. We are happy to serve him, why not? He will make a better king than Aethelred."

Ironsides' father, with his dithering, had been nicknamed the Unready.

"So this place is yours and you must enter it proudly. Take your cap off, lift up your head. Comb out your hair and show that fire."

Aelfric was laughing at him. Ed grinned back. It was true – having been in hiding for so long, he was becoming used to skulking along, head down.

"Your scars are battle scars – they will be mightily impressed."

Yes, Ed thought – his battle with Ohtar.

But Ohtar was now far away and what Fric was saying was true – this place was his to command. It helped to throw the old cap away and feel the wind in his ears again.

"And Estrid – Queen Estrid!"

They capered about on the hilltop, glad to be at the end of the gruelling journey. It was hard to make themselves smart but they tried. Estrid tugged her comb through the Firehead curls, and then Hilde undid Estrid's long braids and combed out her rather dirty hair.

"The first thing we'll do is get clean,"

Estrid declared as she was waited on. "And order some new clothes."

But perhaps their new retainers would recognize that beneath the grime of travel their clothes were fine and expensive. Estrid had no difficulty at all in behaving like a proud queen; it was her birthright. Ed hoped her attitude would rub off on him. It was a pity they had no horses, but that couldn't be helped.

"There are no young men left here," Fric said. "Only old men, too old to fight, and women. If you don't upset them, they'll be happy enough to serve you. They are lucky still to be unharmed. There's been plenty of fighting round here. Many of the settlements were burnt out and all the cattle taken to feed the armies. These people are lucky."

"I don't mind hard work," Ed said. He knew how a farm should be run, at least, having worked for Ragnar over the years. He doubted if Wistan did.

Fric, more experienced at ordering people about, went first. Ed followed nervously. From slave to master in such a few weeks was a hard act. He tried to think how the old men would feel, turning over their home to a fifteen-year-old stranger. Impossible! And the old women round the hearth, having to take orders from Estrid! He thought they would be outraged. He would say nothing, he thought, but work at the jobs he knew, milk cows, put pigs out to pasture, keep his head down till Wistan returned.

He had not reckoned on the response of the old people to the sight they presented, entering the gateway on that crisp winter morning. It was true they were tired and travel-stained. But Ed walked boldly, holding Estrid by the hand, and their striking looks, the livid scars (of battle, so the viewers thought) and the unmistakable rapport of the radiant partnership between them stopped the old retainers in their tracks. They had expected a posse of soldiers and horses and terse commands. And instead they had these two children, hand in hand. Fric and Hilde gave the orders. Ed and Estrid stood and smiled. The people recognized Aelfric, Wistan's steward.

The women came forward timidly, inviting them into the longhouse. The fire was blazed up, honeycakes and ale offered, a pig put on to roast. The women took Estrid to their quarters to bathe, and Ed asked to be taken round the pastures and see the bounds of the land. An old, one-armed man took him, the grandfather of the fallen sons. At first he was silent, bitter and hostile. But as he gradually came to realize Ed's understanding of the business of farming, he opened up and spoke proudly of his crops and animals. He even admitted that the sons had preferred fighting to farming.

"Young people go looking for adventure. I did too once." He shrugged his half an arm. "Look where it gets you. And you too – you went fighting from the look of you?"

"I had no choice. I went as a slave. My family lost our own farm long ago to the invaders. I know how it feels."

And the old man laughed. His relief at getting Ed, instead of someone like Ohtar, shone out of his watery old eyes.

Strangely, Ed sensed a kinship in this place that made him feel at home. These people were Saxons like his own, not the Norsemen he had grown up with. There was a rooted feel about the place, a softness in the air that was different from the biting eastern shore he was used to. He walked back slowly along the river, enjoying the scene, the clear water with its streaming rushes, the rich grass, no dank smell of tidal mud. It was hard to take in, that this was Wistan's, his. After the tribulations of the past few weeks he felt he was in a dream from which he would awake. The change of fortune was too sudden to take in.

Later in the day when he went into the longhouse he found Estrid amongst the women and girls, laughing and relaxed. She was dressed in new clothes, her gold hair loose and shining, her arms covered in jewelled bracelets. Her eyes were dancing with pleasure at her reception. Ed felt unable to approach her, dirty and tired as he was, seated with the old men at the board. He had to drink and yarn like a leader. The women knew they were not married, and they were to be kept apart until such time as they were.

So Ed knew no longer his intimacy with Estrid. He worked on the farm, and Estrid worked with the women, cooking and weaving and playing with the children and learning to speak their language. Ed felt his way with the new people, said little, waiting for Wistan's return.

Chapter 19

When Wistan returned he came with the news that Ohtar was still searching high and low for Estrid. He said she was in danger, must stay hidden and change her name, and Aelfric must be her bodyguard. He would stay on the farm for the time being until Cnut had need of him.

Travellers passing along the Roman Ridgeway above the farm often came down to the longhouse at night to beg a meal and ask permission to sleep in the granary. On these occasions Wistan forbade Estrid to emerge from the women's quarters. Estrid was angry, liking to meet new faces and hear news from Glastonbury or Lundenberg.

"You make me a prisoner in my own home," she challenged him.

"By all means come and make yourself known. But don't be surprised if one day the visitor is your brother Ohtar. I would have no power to stop him taking you."

Wistan was so strong and forthright that Ed sometimes wondered if Estrid might falter in her love for him and transfer it to his brother. His personality was magnetic, everyone ran to do his bidding and revered him, Ed included. As a man of twenty he had the bearing of a leader, with a fine-boned but already lined face and flecks of grey already in his curling dark hair. He was a restless man, always on the move, graceful and quick, eyes alert for every detail. A natural leader, Ed acknowledged, and was doubtful how he could compare in a girl's eyes.

But Wistan said, "You are the master here, Firehead. This is a working farm and I know nothing of farming. The old men are happy with your expertise."

"Yes, I know the job. Slaves learn fast," Ed said, bitter now at what he saw as competition.

But Wistan smiled.

"I will not get in your way. I have to return to court when Cnut comes back to the West. But remember, you cannot rest from Ohtar's threat. If I can, I will try to overturn Ohtar."

"Overturn?"

Wistan laughed. "A good word – it's your

own guess as to what it means. A chance might come. He's much hated, not just by you and his sweet sister. You're not safe, Firehead, while Ohtar breathes."

Ed did not like to hear what he already knew from his brother's lips. Wistan was always right.

By chance Ed discovered the cruel strength of his purpose.

A traveller came one evening before dark: a youngish man, not poor, but well dressed for his journey and with a pack of provisions. He asked for a night's shelter from the rain and was invited to the board. Ed noticed how his eyes roved over the place, heard the questions he asked. He stared directly at Ed and took in the flaming hair and the bright scars, and asked how he came by such cuts. Ed answered tersely, "In battle." He felt uneasy about this man, and saw Wistan's sharp eyes raking him across the table. Wistan said nothing. The man went to sleep in the hay-barn.

When Ed got up at dawn as usual and went out to see to feeding the cows, he found Wistan and Aelfric in the yard holding Aelfric's horse. No one else was around. Wistan had a sword at his belt, unsheathed. Its tip dripped blood. Ed stopped in his tracks, suddenly cold. He heard Wistan laugh. Aelfric went into the hay-barn and came out backwards dragging the inert body of the young traveller who had sat at the board the previous evening. A thick trail of blood marked his passing. The two men lifted the body over the horse's back so that it hung face down, and fastened it to the saddle with a rope, and then Aelfric took the rein and led the horse away.

"Tip it in the forest," Ed heard Wistan say. "Cover it well."

He then put his sword in the water trough and swished it about, dried it on the hem of his tunic and pushed it back in its scabbard. He kicked loose straw and dust over the trail of blood and came back towards the longhouse, whistling. He didn't see Ed.

Ed said nothing about it. Wistan's nonchalance amazed him, that he could take a life with so little distress, yet he knew that his brother had acted for him. He thought the young man had been Ohtar's spy. He had done him a kindness! Yet they could not live in hiding for ever.

Later Wistan spoke of the possibility of Estrid going back to her father and facing up to his decision on whom she should marry.

"It could be that he might agree to the union now you have this place to offer her. It might not be the whole of Mercia, but it is peaceful and rich enough for a girl of her station. And then he would order Ohtar to give up his enmity towards you and Ohtar would have to obey him."

"Perhaps we should do that." Ed trusted Ragnar's sense of justice and his essential kindness.

"We'll think on it. We'll need a strong band of men for the journey. It will take some planning."

And with that Ed had to be content.

But before this plan could be put into action, a messenger came from Cnut demanding Wistan's presence in Lundenberg. It was just before Christmas. Wistan assumed it was to do with the festivities. Cnut was going to make a big show in church, to show what a good Christian king he was.

Already bored on his estate, Wistan cheered up instantly.

"Come with me, young Firehead! Aelfric, too, as your bodyguard. You don't want to miss out on a feast like this."

"What about leaving Estrid unguarded?"

"She'll not be unguarded. I will leave men here to guard her, and put the whole place on alert. No one will be admitted. I will leave strict orders."

"Ohtar will be with Cnut?"

"I dare say. But he will not dare harm you when I am there. You can look him in the face, hold up your head. Spit in his eye." He laughed. "We could visit Ragnar too, before we come home. It would be a good chance."

Ed was torn about going, but Wistan's excitement was infectious. It would not harm him, after all, to make acquaintance with those that held power. And the bonus of visiting Ragnar decided him. If Ragnar would give his consent – !

Ed's separation from Estrid in this so well-ordered community plagued him with longing. Every day she seemed to grow lovelier and more desirable. He could only send her longing glances across the board, or catch her for a moment's chat when she was about her women's business, never alone. He would have done better to have wooed funny Hilde, who had far more freedom. He might as well have been a slave again, he thought, for all the authority he held amongst the women.

Wistan got him new clothes and accoutrements – a bronze helmet and a chased breastplate, and a new, light sword with a jewelled scabbard. Best of all was a kind-natured horse with smooth paces. Wistan rode like a man born in the saddle. Ed envied him.

Even Aelfric rode better than he did. And Estrid.

They set out with a bodyguard of some dozen men, proudly mounted. In three days they reached Lundenburg and found a much happier place than the one they had left. A year away from the eternal siege, the Lundenburg people had accepted the Danish presence and got on with their trading and money-making. They knew that Cnut was still working out the exact price they were going to have to pay in silver as retribution for their resistance, and they knew it would be enormous. But in spite of that spirits were high. Peace was a novelty, and they were enjoying it.

Cnut was staying in the royal precinct at Aldermanbury and his retainers were lodged in various houses nearby. Prayers and celebrations took place in the Minster of St Paul's and the churches of All Hallows and St Andrews, and in the evening drinking and feasting took place round the groaning boards in the court residences. The celebrations seemed to have more to do with getting drunk than thanking God. But half the Danes were still pagans and no doubt were privately paying homage to their old gods, Thor, Odin, Ty and company who had done them so proudly in war.

Once again Ed, although excited by the crowds and pomp, was glad he was not a courtier or soldier. He waited to hear exactly why Wistan had been summoned, and was surprised when Wistan came back from an audience with Cnut looking disturbed and excited.

"What did he want?"

Ed wanted whatever it was to be over so that they could ride on to Essex to speak to Ragnar.

Wistan took Ed out of the hall and into a quiet street under the wall.

"It's a serious business. Maybe you should have stayed at home."

"But you're going to tell me what it is?"

"Yes. Because it has to do with Eadric Streona – and Ohtar."

He looked at Ed in the pale winter sunlight, put out a hand and touched one of Ed's scars. Ed stared up at him, curious.

"You can have a chance now, to make amends. For your face, for Sigy – "

"How? What is it?"

"You'll not mention this to anyone, not Aelfric or anyone else? I trust you implicitly. You swear on it?"

"Yes, I swear to God."

"Cnut has commanded a band of us, six of

his most trusted men, to assassinate someone who displeases him. Perhaps you can guess who it is?"

"Ohtar?" Ed breathed, his eyes shining.

"No. Ohtar is small fry. It is Eadric Streona."

Ed felt his jaw drop. The king of Mercia! Not some petty money-thief, but one of the highest in the land. And the most blatant traitor of the lot. All his life Eadric had insinuated himself with whoever was winning, changing sides like thistledown in a breeze.

"Cnut has to go back to Denmark to secure his kingdom there, and he cannot leave anyone here who is not trustworthy. The plan is to take him after the feasting on Christmas Day, when he goes back to his quarters. Whoever is with him will be killed too, whether they deserve it or not. I am pretty sure one of those by his side will be Ohtar. This is why I am telling you this. That you may be there. It would repay you for the wrongs he has done you."

Wistan's eyes were shining with excitement at the task ahead of him. Ed, recalling vividly the bloodshed on the battlefield, felt his gorge rise with his own sick excitement. Ohtar! He nodded his head.

"Yes!"

Would he rise to it? He was hardly practised.

Wistan laughed. "Were you not hardened at Assunden? If you'd fought in more battles this would be nothing to you. Why do you think I am still alive? Because I killed the other before he killed me. I fought in six battles, first with Aethelred, then with Ironsides. And no one ever wounded me."

Christmas Day dawned dark and heavy with rain. It was bitterly cold. Smoke from hundreds of fires was shredded away on the wind and the marshes were flooded beyond the wall, home to flocks of geese from foreign shores. Ed shivered under his woollen fleece on the bench, trembling with excitement for what the day would bring. The soldiers of the guard were already drinking, and slaves were dishing out wooden platters of porridge from the hearth. The king was to attend a mass at the Minster of St Paul's in the morning and they were to accompany him. They had to be brushed and combed and clean, fit to attend a king, and they would get very wet. The mud was knee-deep by the Minster.

In spite of the weather a fair crowd turned out to watch the procession and the Minster was crowded to the doors as Cnut entered. He wore a gold, jewelled crown and his blond hair curled down to his shoulders. He was surrounded by his bodyguard and followed by the kings of Mercia and East Anglia and Northumbria and all their entourage. Flaring torches illuminated the dark wooden building, glinting on gold jewellery and silver sword hilts. The bishops came in, in even more finery than the king, and the monks chanted, their breath steaming in clouds on the cold air, their bare blue feet padding on the stone floor. Ed was pushed and jostled, standing at Wistan's shoulder in the aisle. He knew Cnut was a great king, the greatest since Alfred, and he was seeing history made, but he wished he were at home with Estrid by the hearth with the old aunties ordering the cooking of meat and honeycakes and the flames dancing in Estrid's eyes. He was frightened for Wistan, tonight, and himself too, if the truth were known.

After the service Cnut came down the centre of the church and they stood back to let him pass. As he came to Wistan, Ed saw that they exchanged glances, and Cnut nodded his head fractionally, and passed on. The wet crowd cheered, the banners lifted themselves heavily in a gust of sleet, and he passed on out of sight.

In the evening they went to the Christmas

Night feast in the royal precinct at Alder-manbury. They wore their finest clothes, their swords and their long cloaks. Wistan was joined by men of Cnut's bodyguard and they sat together at the board, below the king and the aeldermen. Wistan laughed and chatted, but drank nothing. Ed sat near him, with Aelfric. At the top sat Eadric Streona, very confident, smarming up to Cnut who smiled, as two-faced as the famous traitor. Ohtar sat beside him.

It seemed to Ed a very long and tense evening. There were speeches, and a great deal of drinking and shouting, and some of the men fell asleep under the table. The king left early, but Eadric sat on, taking the king's part. When he rose it was very late, and his going was a signal for a general exodus. In the street there was shouting and singing.

Wistan came and took Ed's arm, and told Aelfric to go back to their quarters. He was not a part of the killing. He looked surprised.

"Shall I wait up?"

"We shan't be long."

There were five other men, Cnut's retai-ners, who they joined in the shadow of the old wall.

One of them said, "He has gone to his quar-ters. Northman is with him, and Aethelweard and Beorhtric, and Ohtar. The servants are all asleep."

"We'll wait while they disrobe and put away their swords. But before the torches are put out, we'll go in. Waste no time. They must all be killed."

They went down the street in the dark to the doorway of the old Cripplegate building, a remainder of Roman times. Over the gateway was a long guardroom which was being used as accommodation by Eadric's party. Torch-light glowed in the wall openings above. A bitter breeze blew down the street, and the old trees beyond the wall bent and creaked, scraping the stones.

The small party crept up the stone staircase, Ed last of all. He could not believe this moment had come. He was shaking with eagerness, his heart beating so hard he thought it would warn Eadric of their coming. The men moved noiselessly, sliding their swords from their scabbards. They came to the doorway, and saw the embers glowing in the hearth in the middle of the floor and the figures of Eadric and his friends silhouetted against the fire. They were pulling out their fleeces, about to lie down, and their shadows danced across the far wall.

"Come," Wistan said.

The shadows turned. The men moved so quickly, noiselessly, that Ed hardly saw what happened. He heard dreadful sounds, gurgling, gasping, a strangled shout, sobbing. A scream cut off abruptly. Silence. The professionalism stunned him.

"Firehead!" Quite softly.

He searched for the voice, stepped over two sprawled bodies.

Wistan held Ohtar against a buttress in the stone wall with his sword across Ohtar's neck. Ohtar could not move without cutting his own throat. Wistan stood easily, in perfect command.

"Kill him," he said to Edmund. "He is yours."

Ed lifted his sword, waited. He looked straight into Ohtar's eyes, and saw the flames of the fire flickering there. And fear. Stark, blind fear. He knew he had never shown Ohtar that fear, and nor had Sigy. He did not hurry, staring, drinking in Ohtar's fear. He knew he was smiling. Ohtar could see his smile.

Wistan misunderstood his delay.

"Kill him," he said. "He is yours."

He waited.

"For Sigy," Wistan said.

"Yes. For Sigy," Ed whispered.

And Firehead lifted his sword and stuck it straight into Ohtar's heart. It went in very easily, driven hard by a savage will. The whole weight of Ohtar's body came on Ed's arm and he had to thrust again, to stop the body falling on him. Wistan's sword glittered against the bared throat. Ohtar made a terrible noise and slithered to the ground like a cloak falling off a hook. Ed's sword still stuck out of his chest and he had to pull it free. Wistan put his foot on the slumped body to help him. His own sword had nearly severed Ohtar's head from his body and the sight was so terrible that Ed felt the nausea rising up in his throat. He snatched his sword from Wistan and flung himself away. He dashed to the doorway and rattled down the stone steps into the street to feel the cold draught of sanity on his face. He took great gulps of the icy air. The rest of the men came quickly down behind him, murmuring amongst themselves.

"Are they all dispatched?" Wistan asked. "I took Eadric and Northman. They are certainly dead."

"And I Beorhtric of Devon."

"And I Aethelweard."

Wistan laughed. "And you, Firehead?"

"I took Ohtar," Ed whispered.

It was like taking a prize from the gods, the

greatest they could offer, the sweetness washing over him like the rivers of Ohtar's lifeblood. Ed was dizzy with the feel of it. He had blood all over his clothes and hands, and so did the others. They washed their hands and swords in a running stream and rubbed at the hot stains on their woollen tunics.

"We are to report to the king that it is done," Wistan said. "He said he would wait up."

Ed scarcely remembered the rest of the night, only – somewhere – seeing Cnut in his undervest, smiling – no, laughing – and clasping Wistan's hand. And then his own, and the ice-chip eyes raking him. The gold crown hung on a nail in the wall.

And when they went back to their own quarters, Wistan gave Ed a sword. It was gold-plated and had a serpent chased on the hilt, with topaz eyes. The most beautiful sword Ed had ever seen.

"Ohtar's!"

"No," Wistan said. "Yours."

They went to their cold beds and in a moment Wistan was asleep, sprawled like an innocent baby amongst the warm blankets. Edmund lay stunned, unable to take in what had happened, what he had done. He could not believe that the act of killing had – literally at a stroke – solved all the problems of his life. Revenged dear Sigy. Won him Estrid, settled his fears. The sword was cold at his side. He did not sleep until the first cold light of dawn slipped through the opening.

Chapter 20

Ed rode beside Wistan, along the road he knew so well. The old, familiar smell of the marshes was in his nostrils, the grey sky bitter overhead.

Wistan said, "I found Oswy, you know – it went out of my head to tell you in the little excitement at Aldermanbury. I sent Aelfric out looking, and he came back with word that Oswy was in business horse-trading in Staines, and well and prospering. He fought at Assunden too, and at Aylsford, so we have crossed tracks several times. Perhaps we can offer our parents and our sisters a home at Wanetage later, if they want it. We can see them on our way home."

Ed had passed through Staines with Rollo – how strange to know that his family had been so close! A wash of uncommon affection for his mother and father overtook him – they seemed a hundred years away, not a mere five. He could scarcely remember their faces. It would be weird to meet them again.

As they neared the Norse settlement Wistan said, "We know nothing of Ohtar's death, remember. We have heard of it, of course, no more."

"I killed him." Ed found it hard to come to terms with what had happened.

"You would have been dead long ago if he had had his way. Remember that. When I saved you, by the skin of your teeth ... over Sigy's body – I shall never forget the look on your face as you stood there."

"Of terror?" Ed was puzzled.

"No. Not terror. Defiance, almost triumph. He didn't have the satisfaction of seeing you afraid, as you did him."

"I thought I was going to join Sigy. I wanted to, just then. I wanted him to kill me."

"Time heals. You would not want death now, with all that lies before you."

"No."

But what lay before him? Ragnar's acceptance of his role as son-in-law? With Streona's death, young Streona was no longer a great catch. Everything was in his favour. Yet he dared not believe it. He had stolen Estrid from Ragnar and fled, and the last time he had seen

Ragnar was when Ragnar ordered his flogging. Wistan seemed to have forgotten these details.

At least Ragnar would be impressed by the visitation, if appearances were anything to go by. Wistan had found fine horses and a brave bodyguard. They rode proudly, in clean, rich clothes, with Cnut's banner at their head. Messengers had gone on to prepare Ragnar.

Wistan glanced sideways at his young brother, and thought Ragnar would be a fool to reject him. He laughed.

"Cheer up, young Firehead! It will go well, I promise you."

Ohtar's shadow had lain over Ed ever since he had first set eyes on him. He had been as near death from Ohtar on that first occasion as at any time since. It was hard to accept that the shadow was now dissolved. Ed had never known true freedom before. Not ever. Wistan did not understand how difficult it was to get used to. Every time Ed felt Ohtar's sword heavy against his horse's flank, the vision of Ohtar's staring, terrified eyes came before him, in the last second of his life. He could not get the memory out of his head. How could he laugh, as Wistan laughed?

"We'll hide Ohtar's sword here in this ditch, and collect it on the way home," Wistan said. "Ragnar would know it at once. Take Aelfric's."

Ed had thought that the settlement would be heavy in mourning for Ohtar and that their reception would be unwilling and cold. He thought Ragnar would hate him.

But he had not reckoned on the fact that it was their beloved Rollo who had brought the news of Ohtar's death. And Rollo's arrival had been more a signal for rejoicing than Ohtar's death was a signal for grieving. No one had liked Ohtar, not even his parents. But they loved Rollo.

So when they arrived it was to a reception headed by Rollo, with his parents standing behind him. And Rollo was overjoyed to see Edmund again and made no pretence at hiding it. And his boisterous embrace made Ragnar smile, and then Wistan's easy charm waylaid him. Ragnar never mentioned the occasion of his last meeting with young Firehead.

The feast was laid on, the wine flowed and the fire-shadows leapt in the longhouse. Wistan, for all the wine, never lost track of the purpose of the visit and led the conversation cleverly to the business between Estrid and Edmund. Ragnar followed him closely, trying to resist this persuasive young Saxon. But he could find no flaw in Wistan's argument. And Wistan was now a close retainer of Cnut's, with as much influence as the deposed Streona.

Wistan said, "Estrid lives with the ladies at my estate, awaiting your permission to marry Edmund. We have come to ask your blessing, and show you what we can offer her."

He set out the deal to Ragnar and his lady. He had three estates, and was no farmer by inclination. They could visit them all, and they could take one for their own if they preferred it, and Edmund and Estrid could take another. The country was at peace; Cnut was his friend and he owned wealth from battle which would see them all content.

Ragnar's tired blue eyes travelled from Wistan's cool gaze to Ed's eager, trembling face. He saw the shadow of the defiant young slave behind the scarred face, remembered the courage that had withstood Ohtar's cruelty. It was with relief now that he saw his beloved daughter in the arms of this brave young Firehead, and the smile that started to light his face gave the news of his acceptance.

"Estrid is yours."

When Ed lay by Rollo on the bench that night, watching the embers flickering in the hearth, hearing the familiar sea wind whistling over the thatch, he was more content than he could ever remember. The days in Lundenburg had been a nightmare, and he knew that he could never live like Wistan lived. Wistan said he could never be a farmer. So be it. Ed thought of the lovely valley below the downs where Estrid waited for him. And of the moment when Wistan had stayed Ohtar's sword over Sigy's body.

When they departed, he asked Wistan if they could make a detour to the battlefield and see Sigy's grave.

"It's hardly out of our way. And I might not come this way again."

"We'll say some prayers up there. You're not the only one who lost a friend that day."

They picked up Ohtar's sword and Ed thrust it home in his scabbard, where it hung heavily on his horse's flank. They crossed the river and rode across the marshes to the hill where so many men had been killed.

"The king is going to build a church here at Assunden," Wistan said. "To commemorate the dead."

But Edmund's dead was under a wild rose tree and would never be in a church. The rose tree had thrived and tossed bright red hips against the leaden sky. Ed got off his horse and knelt down on the hummocky grass. He was going to be sad, but somehow he felt Sigy was laughing at him. Sigy had always laughed, until the end. Ed's horse was lipping at the tasty hips and Ed had to get up and pull him away. He didn't know whether he was laughing or crying.

The hillside was still scattered with the remains of skeletons, bones picked bare and half grown over now with grass and thistles. Their horses wound their way back down the hill and occasionally crunched a white bone. Ed rode with Aelfric, who recalled his excitement in the battle, his successful thrusts, his near misses, his wild parrying.

They came to the river and dropped into single file to cross the ford. Ed rode at the back, lifting his legs as the ebbing tide swirled around his horse's belly.

On an impulse he snatched Ohtar's sword from its scabbard. He was going home to dear Estrid and the good land, all his fears settled – why did he want a sword which carried so much blood? He had no wish to be a soldier like Wistan. He lifted the sword high, to throw it into the tidal stream. The clear sea water would wash away its history of blood and cruelty. The little topaz eyes glittered in the sun.

His horse stumbled. He laughed, missed his throw.

And then he thought, how could he tell what the gods – or *the* God – might put in his path in the years to come? Sigy had never guessed what tragedy had lain in wait for him. How could he know?

And he slipped the sword back in its scabbard.

One day he might need it.